Whale Song

Cheryl Kaye Tardif

WHALE SONG: School Edition

http://www.cherylktardif.com

FIRST EDITION

Imajin Books

ISBN: 978-1-926997-29-2

Previous print editions:
2010 Imajin Books, revised third edition
2007 Kunati Books; special revised and expanded edition
2003 Trafford Publishing; first debut

Ebook editions also available at various retailers

Cover designed by Sapphire Designs
http://www.designs.sapphiredreams.org

Cover Art: David Miller – http://www.mauiarts.com

Praise for WHALE SONG

"I read *Whale Song* and loved it." —Jodelle Ferland, actress (*The Twilight Saga: Eclipse, Case 39*)

"Tardif's story has that perennially crowd-pleasing combination of sweet and sad that so often propels popular commercial fiction...Tardif, already a big hit in Canada...a name to reckon with south of the border." —*Booklist*

"*Whale Song* is deep and true, a compelling story of love and family and the mysteries of the human heart...a beautiful, haunting novel." —NY Times bestselling novelist Luanne Rice, author of *Beach Girls*

"A wonderfully well-written novel. Wonderful characters [that] shine. The settings are exquisitely described. The writing is lyrical. *Whale Song* would make a wonderful movie." —*Writer's Digest*

"*Whale Song* is reminiscent of *Ring of Endless Light* by M. L'Engle, and *Secret Life of Bees* by Sue Monk Kidd." —Carol D. O'Dell, author of *Mothering Mother*

"One doesn't simply read a Tardif story, one experiences it! Among the very few authors I've ever said that about is my all-time favorite Pat Conroy. Like him, Cheryl Kaye Tardif has a definite way with words." —Betty Dravis, co-author of *Dream Reachers* I & II.

"A powerful, unforgettable story. It is rare that I read a book that moves me so much that I feel compelled to write to the author and her publisher, thanking them for making the book available to be experienced. Whale Song is such a book for me. I was taken on a journey with Sarah Richardson as she experienced loss after loss, yet emerged victorious, wiser, and stronger. This is a story of grief but most of all of the enduring power of love, and of the amazing connections that all beings have with one another." —Beth Fehlbaum, author of *Courage in Patience*

"Tardif leaves a lasting mark on her readers...Moving and irresistible." —*Midwest Book Review*

"*Whale Song* is a moving tale, written in the style of traditional oral story-telling—steeped in the lore and wisdom of Canada's aboriginals." —Eileen Schuh, author of *Schrodinger's Cat*

This special School Edition of Whale Song is dedicated to every young person who has been bullied or discriminated against. Follow your heart and your dreams. Be true to who you are.
I promise you, it gets better.

Acknowledgements

Thank you to everyone who has made Whale Song possible, from family and friends to editors, artists—you know who you are.

And a special thanks to every Whale Song fan who has embraced my "heart book", laughed and cried with my characters, and found a deeper meaning and message within these pages. You inspire me to be a better writer, one who connects with her readers. Thank you.

prologue

I once feared death.

It is said that death begins with the absence of life. And life begins when death is no longer feared. I have stared death in the face and survived. A survivor who has learned about unfailing love and forgiveness. I realize now that I am but a tiny fragment in an endless ocean of life, just as a killer whale is a speck in her immense underwater domain.

It's been years since I've experienced the freedom of the ocean. And years since that one horrifying tragedy took away everything and everyone that I loved. I have spent my life fighting my fragmented memories, imprisoned by guilt and betrayal. I had stopped hoping, dreaming or loving.

I was barely alive.

Locked away in darkness, I struggled—until I learned the lessons from Seagull, Whale and Wolf.

Now I am free.

I finally remember my youth. I recall the happy times, the excursions in the schooner and the sunlight reflecting off deep blue water. I can still visualize the mist of water spouting from the surface and a ripple opening to release the dorsal fin of a killer whale.

But what I remember most is the eerie, plaintive song of the whale, caught on the electronic sound equipment of the research schooner. Her song still lingers in my mind.

A long-forgotten memory…

PART ONE

Village of the Whales

one

In the summer of 1977, my parents and I moved from our rambling ranch home in Wyoming to Vancouver Island, Canada. My father had been offered a position with *Sea Corp,* a company devoted to studying marine life. He would no longer be a marine biology professor at the university. Instead, he'd be studying killer whales and recording their vocalization.

My mother was ecstatic about the move. She couldn't wait to return to Canada where her parents were living. She chatted nonstop about all the new things we would see and do.

But I was miserable. I didn't want to move.

"You'll make new friends, Sarah," my parents told me.

But I—like most eleven-year-old girls—hated them for making me leave the friends I already had.

Since our new home was fully furnished, we were leaving almost everything behind. A few personal belongings, my mother's art supplies and some household items would follow in a small moving van.

My father told us he had rented out our ranch to a nice elderly couple. I was quite happy that no children were going to be living in my bedroom, but I was miserable about leaving behind my prized possessions. I reluctantly said goodbye to my little bed, my Bay City Rollers wall posters, my bookshelf of Nancy Drew mysteries, my mismatched dresser and my swimming trophies. Then I sulked on the edge of the bed and watched my mother sift through my things.

"I know it's hard," she said, catching my sullen mood. "Think of this as an adventure."

I let out an angry huff and flopped onto my back.

"I don't want an adventure."

The following morning, we left Wyoming with my three-speed bike strapped to the roof of the car and our suitcases and my mother's easel piled in the trunk. That night, I watched TV in a motel room while my parents talked about our new home in Canada.

"Time for bed, Sarah," my father said after a while. "We have a long day ahead of us tomorrow."

Unable to sleep, I tossed restlessly in the bed and stared at the ceiling, wondering what life would be like stuck on a tiny island.

How boring it's going to be.

I thought of Amber-Lynn MacDonald, my best friend back in Wyoming. She was probably crying her eyes out, missing me. Who was I going to tell all my secrets to now?

I swallowed hard, fighting back the tears.

Life is so unfair.

Little did I know just how unfair life could be.

It felt like days later when we finally arrived in Vancouver. We drove to the ferry terminal and waited in a long lineup of vehicles. We boarded the ferry and I rushed to the upper deck where I stood against the rails and watched the mainland disappear. The water was choppy and the ferry swayed side-to-side. When we saw Vancouver Island approaching, dismal gray clouds greeted us and I instantly missed the scorching dry heat of Wyoming.

The drive from the ferry terminal to our new house took hours and seemed relentlessly slow. After a while, we veered off the highway and headed along the main road to Bamfield. The narrow unpaved road was bumpy and pitted. It was swallowed up by massive, intimidating logging trucks that blasted their horns at us.

I watched them roll precariously close while my father steered our car until it hugged the side of the road. I held my breath, waiting for the huge bands that secured the logs to snap and release the lumber onto our car. And I was sure that we'd topple over into the ditch or onto the rocks below.

I released a long impatient breath. "Where's the ocean?"

"You just saw it," my father chuckled. "From the ferry."

"No, I mean the *ocean* ocean," I muttered. "That was just like a big lake. I want to see the *real* ocean, where it stretches out for miles and you can't see the end of it."

My mother turned and smiled. "You just wait. You'll see it soon enough."

I settled into the back seat with my latest Nancy Drew book and tried to read. But my eyes kept wandering to the window. When we hit a huge pothole, my book dropped to the car floor. It stayed there for the remainder of the trip.

I pushed my face against the window and watched the scenery streak past. The forest that surrounded us was enormous and forbidding. Moss hung eerily from damp branches and a fog danced around the tree trunks.

Then the sun broke out from behind a cloud—free at last from its dark imprisonment. It quickly heated up the interior of the car. Unfortunately, the gravel road kicked up so much dust that I wasn't allowed to roll down the window. And since we didn't have air conditioning, my hair—or my *Italian mane* as my mother called it—hung limply to my waist and my bangs stuck to my forehead.

I scowled. We'd been driving for days and I was tired of being cooped up in the car.

"Close your eyes, Sarah," my father said, interrupting my thoughts. "And don't open them 'til I say."

I obeyed and held my breath in anticipation.

I'm finally going to see the ocean.

Minutes ticked by and I grew restless. Being a typical eleven-year-old, I had to sneak a peek.

"Okay, now you can look," my father said.

He chuckled when he caught me with my eyes already open.

Pushing my damp bangs aside, I scrunched my face up close to the window. The ocean was spread out before me, interrupted only by a tiny island here and there. The water's surface was choppy with whitecaps and it looked dark and mysterious.

I smiled, satisfied.

Back in Wyoming, we saw endless stretches of green hills and grass with mountains rising in the distance. That was all I'd ever known. I could go horseback riding and never see water bigger than our duck pond. Now before me, the ocean seemed to go on endlessly.

I couldn't resist rolling down the window. As soon as I did, I heard waves crashing along the shoreline.

"Well, what do you think?" my father asked. "This road winds all along the shore. Every now and then, you'll be able to see the ocean. And once we reach Bamfield, our house is just east of town, right on the water."

He reached over and tugged at a piece of my mother's long auburn hair. I laughed when she swatted his hand.

"The house will be ours for the next three years," my mother said over her shoulder. "It belongs to an older couple, so we'll have to take very good care of it."

Twenty minutes later, we passed a sign. *Welcome to Bamfield.*

I breathed a sigh of relief. We were almost there.

As we drove unnoticed through the modest town, I realized that it was much smaller than Buffalo, the town nearest our ranch in Wyoming. After stopping at *Myrtle's Restaurant & Grill* for a delicious supper of deep-fried halibut and greasy home-style French fries, we clambered back into the car and headed for our new home.

"The house is just up ahead," my father said. "I know you're going to love it, Dani."

He gave my mother a long, tender look.

My mother, Daniella Andria Rossetti, was born and raised in San Diego, California. Her parents were immigrants from Italy who had moved to the United States after World War II.

When she was eighteen, her parents moved again—this time to Vancouver, Canada. My mother took advantage of the move, left home and struck out for Hollywood with hopes of becoming a famous actress. After numerous rejections and insulting offers from sleazy directors, she gave up her stalled acting career and studied art and oil painting instead. Within a few months, her work was shown at *Visions*, a popular art gallery in San Francisco.

It was there that she met my father.

Jack Richardson was a Canadian marine biology student who had wandered in off the street after being caught in a tempestuous downpour of rain. Six months later, my mother moved in with him—much to her parents' disapproval. Four months went by and they were married in a small church with a few friends and family present.

During the next three years, my parents tried to have a child. They had almost given up hope when they discovered that my mother was pregnant. Six months into a perfect pregnancy, she miscarried. My parents were devastated.

Eight months later, my father's stepfather and mother were killed in a car accident. During the reading of the will, my father discovered that he had inherited the family ranch in Wyoming.

But my mother was upset. She didn't want to leave the bustling city of San Francisco for the wide-open plains near Buffalo. When the curator of *Visions*, Simon McAllister, promised that she could courier her paintings to the gallery, my mother agreed to the move.

After a year on the ranch, she couldn't imagine living anywhere else. Her work thrived, reflecting images of country living, meadows and mountains. Then she was rewarded with unbelievable news. She was pregnant again.

Nine months plus a week later Sarah Maria Richardson weighed in at eight pounds, four ounces. At three months old, I had thick black hair and dark brown eyes. My parents doted on me.

When I was about six, my mother told me how handsome my father had looked the moment she first saw him in the art gallery. Even though he was shivering and drenched, he had stared at one of her paintings for the longest time.

WHALE SONG

My mother had fallen in love with him that instant.

It sounded like a fairytale to me, but I believed that my parents loved each other and that they would be together.

Forever.

Now years later, we were driving along the rustic coast of Vancouver Island, anticipating the first glance of our new home. I felt restless and uneasy. I somehow knew that my life would change the second we drove into those trees.

Destiny...or fate?

As the sun began to set overhead, we reached a small, barely legible sign that read *231 Bayview Lane*. A gravel driveway curved and disappeared into the trees. When the car followed it, we were plunged into darkness. Branches reached out to the car roof, caressing it like a thousand hungry fingers.

The tall cedar trees that surrounded the car opened to reveal a lush lawn carefully landscaped with small shrubs. At the end of the gravel driveway, a two-story cedar house stood just beyond the lawn. The shingles of the roof gleamed in the reddening sunlight. The main door into the house was solid wood with no window. In fact, there were only three small windows on that entire side of the house.

Our new home seemed forlorn—empty.

"Well, not much to look at from here," my mother mumbled. "But I'm sure it's much nicer inside. We could always punch out a window...or two."

My father grinned. "Dani, my love, looks can be deceiving. Just wait until you see inside."

When he pulled the car onto a cement pad, my mother smirked. "The garage?" she asked sarcastically.

"You're so funny," he said, unfolding himself from the driver's seat.

I clambered out, impatient to get inside and explore. Reaching for his hand, I tugged on it and pulled him toward the house while my mother followed behind.

At the door, we turned back and caught sight of her pale face.

"Are you okay?" my father asked.

"I'm just a bit carsick," she said with a wry smile. "You two go in first, let me get some fresh air. I'll be in shortly."

"If you're—"

She laughed. "Go inside, Jack. I'm okay."

With a shrug, my father unlocked the door and gave it a gentle nudge. Then he turned to me, his mouth widening into the biggest smile I had ever seen.

"Welcome to your new home, Sarah," he said.

I let go of his hand and eagerly stepped inside, a thrill of excitement racing

through me. "I want to see my roo—"
    I froze, dead in my tracks.

two

It was the dazzling light that hit us first.

Large picture windows wrapped the entire front of the house and faced the ocean. The flaming sunset outside made the interior glow like the embers of a fire.

"Wow," I murmured.

My eyes swept across the open main floor. There was a living room to my left. It was decorated in bronze and copper tones, and two beige plaid couches framed a chocolate-brown area rug. To my right, a dining room table and four chairs claimed the area in front of one of the windows.

I ran to it, almost knocking over a potted plant. I looked out the window and stared, mesmerized, as the setting sun sparkled on the bay.

"I can hear the ocean, Dad."

The door behind us opened and my mother joined us, her face instantly lighting up. "It's beautiful, Jack."

"It's private too," my father said. "The nearest neighbor is about a fifteen-minute walk down the beach." He teasingly ruffled my hair. "Hey, do you want to check out the rest of the house?"

"Do I ever," I said, my eyes wide with anticipation.

He led me to a large closet by the back door. "This is the closet." His voice was serious, as if he were a realtor showing me a potential property.

I laughed. "No kidding, Dad."

I took off my jacket and hung it in the empty space. That was my first claim on my new home.

"Over here is the living room," my father said with a sweep of one hand.

I pointed to a large black monstrosity. "What is *that* thing?"

My mother stifled a gasp. "A wood-burning stove. How charming. I love it, Jack." She spun on her heel slowly and surveyed the room. "You were right about this house. It's perfect for us."

I agreed. The house was far better than I had expected.

I walked closer to the stove.

Over it, a cedar shelf was mounted to the peach-colored wall. On it was a peculiar collection of oddities—an eagle's feather, a fisherman's glass ball wrapped with twine, a skull from a small animal and a crab shell.

I looked up and gasped. "Mom! That's your painting."

The large watercolor that hung above the shelf was the one my mother had painted while she was pregnant with me. It was of a mountain waterfall and was her very favorite. Mine too.

"I sent it on ahead so it would be here when we arrived," my father explained. "I asked the caretaker to hang it. He also made sure we have lots of firewood. And he turned the electricity back on too."

"Let's check out the kitchen," my mother said, rubbing her hands gleefully.

A spacious country kitchen with a wooden island was tucked around the corner, barely visible. The walls were painted the palest sage green and along the ceiling edge ran a soft leafy border. A small round table and two chairs sat in one corner.

My mother busied herself by checking out the fully stocked cupboards and making a pot of tea while I continued my exploration of the lower level of the house. Between the kitchen and dining room area, a wrought iron staircase led to the upper floor. Behind the stairs, a sliding glass door opened onto a cedar deck.

"Can I go out there?" I asked my father.

He smiled. "Of course. It's your house now."

We stepped outside and the humid night air enveloped us.

"Hey," I shouted. "A swinging chair."

The deck held a padded swing, big enough for three people. There was also a barbecue and a picnic table with two benches. A protective wooden rail ran around the entire deck, with an opening for the stairs that led to the ground below.

I leaned over the rail.

A well-trodden rocky path led from the bottom of the stairs, through the grass and down to the beach. From the deck, I saw waves crashing on the fiery shore. Better yet, I heard them. I breathed in the salty air, thrilled with my new home.

Then I turned and darted inside, urging my father to follow.

"Come on, Dad," I yelled. "I want to see my room."

He smiled and remained where he was. "You two go ahead."

Grabbing my mother's hand, I raced up the spiral staircase to the upper floor. Under my pounding feet, the stairs groaned with a dull *clang*. I turned down the hall and entered the first room on the right.

9

WHALE SONG

The room was tiny—like a baby's nursery. But there was no crib. There wasn't even a bed. The walls were painted off-white, but looked like they had definitely seen better days. Small tables, old toys and cardboard boxes littered the floor. A rocking chair sat motionless near a large window and an antique bookshelf took up one wall. Dusty encyclopedias and ancient books inhabited the shelves.

I drew a heart in the dust.

"This room needs a good cleaning," my mother muttered.

I yanked back my hand and eyed her suspiciously. I was positive that she had plans for me—plans that included a dust rag in one hand and lemon furniture polish in the other.

"This'll be my studio," she said, eying the room.

I barged past her out into the hall. "I want to see *my* room."

The next room I entered boasted a large brass bed with down-filled pillows and a flowered quilt. Along the side walls stood two white colonial dressers, one with a large oval mirror. The other wall had a cedar bench seat built into a bay window that faced the ocean.

I fell in love with that room immediately.

I turned, fingers crossed behind my back. "Is this *your* room?"

I fervently hoped it was not.

My mother looked around the room and pointed to the boxes stacked to one side. On the bottom box, the letter *S* had been scribbled in red marker.

"Looks like it's yours, Honey-Bunny."

I rolled my eyes at her.

My parents had been calling me that ridiculous nickname since I was a baby, but I didn't have the heart to ask them to stop.

Looking around my new room, I was elated. It was twice the size of the one back home, the bed was huge and I could see the ocean from my window.

"I love it, Mom," I said stifling a yawn.

After I took a peek at my parents' room and the large upstairs bathroom, I followed my mother down to the kitchen where I devoured a piece of toast with peanut butter and maple syrup. All through my snack, I wrestled with exhaustion, afraid that I would miss something wonderful. My mother noticed and sent me to bed early.

That was the first time I didn't argue.

In my beautiful ocean room, I sat in the window seat and cranked open the side panel. I heard waves lapping softly against the shore. In the distance, a water bird cried out, searching for his home.

I didn't know it then, but I had found mine.

Everything in the new house was perfect. But I missed Amber-Lynn. I had promised her that I would call and write to her every week. After all, best friends were hard to find. We'd been inseparable since we were two years old. Her parents and mine had often played cards together while the two of us stayed up past midnight watching movies until we fell asleep.

Now I was hundreds of miles away from my friend, but I pledged my undying devotion to her. My only consolation was that in three years I'd be returning to Wyoming, to my ranch and to Amber-Lynn.

Three years.

To a child my age, three years was a lifetime.

As the moon dipped lower behind the trees, I climbed into my new bed and sniffed the spring-fresh sheets.

Then I sank into a dreamless sleep.

"Can I go outside?" I asked my father the next morning.

We were eating breakfast while my mother slept in.

"Sure. Let's go for a walk."

I followed him onto the deck, down the stairs and across the rocky trail to the beach. The sun gleamed off his blond hair, highlighting a few gray ones. At forty-one, my father was the most handsome man I knew. And I loved him more than I loved anyone in the world. He was my idol. He always made my mother and I laugh. He'd pretend he understood the creatures of the sea and he'd tell us what they thought of his fellow professors. Apparently, some of the whales didn't have too many nice things to say about them.

I studied my father as he leaned forward and picked up a rock. He examined it with what my mother and I called his *scientific mind*. Then he skipped it across the water.

When I tried to mimic him, my rock sank with a *thud*.

"Like this," he said.

He showed me how to select a flat stone and fling it toward the water's surface like a Frisbee.

"You have to throw it hard, but keep it flat."

I practiced skipping stones until my arm ached.

"Last one," I said, frustrated.

I flung a smaller stone and to my amazement, it skipped.

One…two…three times.

"You did it!" my father cheered.

We followed the beach a few yards from our house. The shoreline of multi-colored rocks disappeared and a sandy beach curved toward the water.

I squealed with delight and pointed to a floating raft anchored maybe fifteen yards out into the water. "Is that ours?"

11

WHALE SONG

My father's eyes turned serious and dark. "This is all part of our property. It's safe to swim out to the raft, just don't go any farther."

I looked out over the water and noticed an island not too far away. My father stared at it too and I wondered what he was thinking. It wasn't until after supper that I found out.

That was when he told me the story of Fallen Island.

"Last year, the son of one of our neighbors tried to swim out to Fallen Island," he began. "The story I heard was that the boy challenged his younger sister to swim from the raft to the island. When she refused, he went anyway. They say he made it most of the way across." He paused and I clung to my chair, waiting.

"No one knows if he got caught in an old fishing net or if he just got too tired," he continued. "His sister tried swimming out to him, but I guess she panicked and went back to the raft. Her parents found her an hour later, sitting on it, staring at the island."

"Did they find the boy?" I asked.

My father shook his head. "Search teams dragged the bay, but they never found his body. I heard that his sister went to the beach every day for months, hoping to catch sight of her brother. She believed he was still alive. He was only fourteen."

"That's an awful story," my mother moaned. She turned and patted my back. "Your dad never should have told you."

"There's a reason I did," my father argued, looking at me. "I want you to promise, Sarah, that you'll never swim farther than that raft."

There were times when he scared me. And that was one of those times. The intensity of his words combined with his piercing blue eyes made me swallow hard.

"Promise me," he repeated firmly.

As I made that solemn vow, I reminded myself that promises were sacred, not to be broken. I knew that he loved me and that he was only protecting me—or trying to.

My father would always be my protector.

The first week went by swiftly. Our days were spent exploring the beach. My mother was happy because my father didn't have to go to work for two weeks. I watched them take off their shoes and run along the water's edge, laughing like children and holding hands. If Amber-Lynn had been there, I would have felt mortified by my parents' display. Since I was the only witness, I just smiled and watched.

During the second week, my father often went into town to get supplies. I'm

12

sure he just wanted to escape all the cleaning my mother had planned. While he was gone, I helped her clean her new studio. We emptied one side of it and made room for her painting supplies. I dusted the numerous books while she washed the floor and stored the owners' boxes in the basement.

By mid-afternoon, the room sparkled and a faint lemony fragrance lingered in the air. As a finishing touch, we placed some candles and an oil lamp on the round table beside the rocking chair.

"There," I said, setting a blank canvas on the easel. "Now you're ready to paint."

My mother shook her head. "Not quite. At least, not that kind of painting."

To my dismay, she pulled out two cans and two large paint rollers. It appeared that the walls were going to get a new coat. Resigned to my fate, I grabbed a roller and started painting. She started on one side and I started on the other—until we met in the middle. By the time we were finished, we were covered in paint and giggling like children.

It's one of my most favorite memories.

"Good job," my mother said, shaking my hand as we admired the finished result. She leaned against the hallway wall. "I'm exhausted. *And* thirsty. How about some ice tea?"

I laughed and raced down the stairs ahead of her.

By the time she reached the deck, I had already set two tall glasses, complete with lemon slices, and a pitcher of ice tea on the picnic table.

I crossed my fingers behind my back. "Can I go swimming?"

My mother stared out at the bay. "I'm really tired, Sarah. I need to lie down for a bit."

"You don't have to come with me," I assured her. "I promise I'll only swim out to the raft. You know I'm a good swimmer."

I knew she was thinking of all the swimming lessons I'd taken at the Buffalo Recreation Center. I was an advanced swimmer, ahead of most kids my age. Not many eleven-year-olds could swim as fast *or* as far as I could. In fact, the last class I'd taken before we moved was with kids two years older than me. I'd even earned a badge for Intermediate Lifesaving.

"Just for two hours," she said with a sigh. "Don't be gone longer than that."

I gulped down my ice tea and checked my watch. *Darn!* It was already two o'clock.

Charging upstairs, I changed into a one-piece bathing suit. When I caught my reflection in the dresser mirror, I stuck out my barely formed chest and scowled. "One day they'll grow."

Pulling my thick dark hair into a quick ponytail, I secured it with an elastic band. Then I grabbed a towel and sprinted downstairs.

WHALE SONG

My mother was still outside. "Be back by four," she warned.

When I reached the bottom of the stairs, I heard her yell after me. "No farther than the raft!"

"Mothers," I muttered beneath my breath.

I made a beeline for the beach across from the raft. Flinging my towel over a log, I quickly removed my sandals and stepped into the warm water. A few pieces of seaweed and something that looked like a bloated onion swirled around my legs. Other than that, the water was clear.

I laughed and plunged in, shocked by the salty taste in my mouth. Swimming toward the raft, I glanced at the forbidden island across the bay. It didn't look so far.

With the cockiness of youth, I grinned. "I could make that."

I floated on my back and stared at the clouds. After a few minutes, I decided to see if I could swim underwater, holding my breath all the way to the raft. I dove under.

When I reached the raft, I pulled myself up the metal stepladder and stretched out on my stomach, smiling. The raft sizzled under the summer sun and I lazily examined its surface. A few swear words had been scratched out with black marker, but I could still read them. I giggled.

As I shifted my gaze, my eyes were drawn to some initials that were carved into the weathered wood. I traced them with one finger. *RD+MC FOREVER!*

I glanced back at the shore, wondering about the owners of the initials. Who were they and where did they live? There were no houses visible, but the beach disappeared around a tree-lined corner.

Maybe there are houses around the bend.

I glanced at my watch. I had lots of time.

Propping my chin on my hands, I admired the view. It was so peaceful—so soothing that it lulled me. I yawned loudly. Cleaning, painting the studio and swimming had made me more tired than I realized. I rested my head on my arms and dozed under the warm rays of the sun. The water lapped against the raft, like a whisper.

"Amber-Lynn...I wish you were—"

Something splashed nearby.

I thought that maybe I was dreaming—until I heard it again and looked up.

I blinked.

Something was sticking out of the water. Seawater sprayed and foamed off a solid black mass as it rose from the depths. Then it sank underwater, out of sight.

I was captivated by the strange spectacle and waited for it to reappear. But I didn't see a thing.

I admit I was a bit nervous about going in the water.

What if it's a shark?

I didn't even know if there were any sharks in the bay. My father had never said anything. But I knew one thing. I couldn't stay on the raft all day.

I pushed myself up on my elbows and strained my neck for a better view.

The bay seemed quiet and demure—until I sensed something moving in the water behind me.

"That was my brother," a voice said.

three

I whirled around and saw a girl about my age treading water near the raft. She had black hair braided into two long plaits and dark eyes that stared at me curiously.

"What do you mean *'your brother'*?" I asked when my voice had returned from the pit of my stomach.

The girl grinned. "He comes back once in a while. To visit."

She swam toward the raft, climbed up and plopped down cross-legged in front of me.

"I'm Goldie," she said. "Goldie Dixon. What's your name?"

She was smaller than I was, and her skin was darker.

"Sarah Richardson," I replied shyly.

I glanced beyond the edge of the raft, wondering if I'd catch a glimpse of her brother.

"Did you see his fluke?" Goldie asked, her face beaming.

Fluke? Of course…

I knew what the black thing was. It was a whale's tail—its fluke. My father had shown me photos of whales from his marine biology class. Some pictures showed the whales' flukes or tails, some showed whales spouting water and one even caught a whale as it breached and rose almost completely out of the ocean.

"So where's your brother?" I asked, looking around the raft.

"He's dead."

My eyes widened with shock. "What?"

Goldie pointed toward the island. "He drowned. Out there."

That's when I recalled the tragic story my father had told me. I had almost convinced myself that he had made it up, just to scare me away from swimming out too far.

"He died last year swimming out to Fallen Island," she continued, as if I weren't even there.

16

"I heard," I said. "My dad told me and my mom about it. I'm really sorry about your brother."

She stared at me with huge dark eyes. "I'm a *Huu-ay-aht First Nations* Indian. Most people call us *Nootka* Indians. Nana told me your family used to live in the United States—in Wyoming."

"Uh-huh," I said. "My dad's Canadian though. My mom and I are American."

"Any Indians in Wyoming?"

I nodded.

I told her that around our ranch, it was common to find an Arapaho Indian buying one of my mother's paintings. We even had a Shoshone live in our barn for a while. He blessed our lands, our garden and my mother in return.

"So why'd you say that was your brother out there?" I asked.

She looked at Fallen Island. "Nootka believe that killer whales are magical and powerful creatures—almost human. One legend says that killer whales would knock over canoes and drag fishermen overboard, down to the *Village of the Whales*. Then the drowned men would turn into whales themselves." She stood slowly. "My brother has become a whale."

She said this simply—as if there were no other explanation.

"What's his name?" I asked as goosebumps dotted my arms.

"Robert."

Finally, the boy from my father's story had a name.

My eyes wandered to the initials engraved on the raft. *R.D.*

Robert Dixon.

Even at such a young age, I understood how much Goldie needed to believe her Nootka legend. It made sense to me at the time. But as I watched her, I felt sorry for her. Her brother was dead. It was that simple.

Goldie jumped into the water. "Have you ever heard of the Haida Indians?" she asked, treading water.

I shook my head.

"The Haida believe that if you see a whale near a town or village, you're really seeing someone who drowned, someone who's trying to talk to his family."

Neither of us said a word. We simply stared at each other in quiet understanding. Then I dove into the water and we swam back to shore. I kept an eye out behind us though, looking for the whale. I think even Goldie knew that I was nervous.

On the beach, we sat down on some driftwood, dried off with our towels and talked about everything that we liked—our favorite foods, music and singers. She was a big fan of Shaun Cassidy. I was hooked on the Bay City Rollers.

I didn't know why, but it was as though I'd known her all my life. Amber-Lynn wouldn't be happy with me. Regardless, I was ecstatic to have met a new friend—even if Goldie did believe her brother was a killer whale.

"You have very dark skin...for a *white* girl," she said, eyeing me. "You sure you're not Indian?"

"My mom's part Italian. She's pretty dark too. My dad, though, he's...uh...light."

"My parents are Nootka. My Nana lives with us too—my grandmother. She's seventy-two years old. I also have a little sister. Shonda. She's five. Do you have any brothers or sisters?"

I told her how my parents had struggled to have children and that when I came along they were so relieved that they decided to have only me. I asked her more about Robert and learned that he, like me, had been an excellent swimmer.

Goldie was very animated when she spoke about him. Her hands moved expressively and I discovered that she was a great storyteller. When she learned that my father was a scientist and was on the island to research killer whales, she grew silent. I knew she was worried about something.

"He won't hurt them, will he?" she asked, biting her lip.

I was stunned by that simple question.

"Of course not. He's here to *study* them, to find out how they communicate with each other and what their sounds mean. He'd never hurt them."

Goldie was relieved. She stared past the raft, searching the water for a sign. I knew she was thinking of her brother.

As we dried ourselves off and proceeded down the beach toward my house, I invited her to come home with me and meet my mother. But she insisted she had to go home to look after her sister while her grandmother cooked supper.

"I'll be here tomorrow," I said. "Where do you live anyway?"

She pointed down the beach and told me that her house was around the bend, just beyond a small dock. I promised her that I'd return the next day.

Then I raced home.

As I sprinted up to the deck and entered through the sliding doors, I glanced at my watch. "Shoot." I was late.

"I'm home," I hollered.

I heard footsteps overhead. "Sarah, is that you?"

"Yeah, Mom."

A minute later she appeared. "I was just about to go look for you. It's almost half past four." She tapped her watch.

"Sorry," I said. "I met an Indian girl when I was swimming and we started talking...and I forgot about the time."

My mother sat down at the dining room table. "What's your friend's name?"

I told her all about Goldie. When I got to the part about her brother, my mother's smile vanished.

"Mom, did you know that some Indians believe that if a person drowns they can come back as a whale?"

"That's a wonderful legend," she replied, her smile returning.

Outside, a car engine rumbled to a stop. A second later, the back door opened and my father appeared.

"Hey," he said. "What have you two been up to all day?"

Before he could take his shoes off, I told him all about Goldie, her brother and the whale in the bay.

"She's afraid you'll hurt the whales," I said.

He patted my hand. "Tell her I'm just studying them. I promise I won't hurt them."

At suppertime, my father told us he had some exciting news.

"*Sea Corp* is getting a new schooner with state-of-the-art electronic equipment. It's coming all the way from Finland."

He was so excited that he couldn't stop talking. He told us that the boat had been built a few years earlier and that one of his co-workers knew the previous owner and had convinced the man to sell it after a year of negotiations.

"We're going to study echolocation," my father said. "Then we'll look at whales' dialects." He turned to me. "Sarah, did you know that whales emit short sounds or clicks?"

I shook my head, trying hard not to laugh at him.

"They listen for the reflecting echo," he continued. "That's how they can tell how far away an object is. Whales measure the time it takes for the echo to return. That's called echolocation."

He loved explaining things to us with his *scientific mind.*

Sometimes my mother would roll her eyes and say, "Here he goes again."

"Killer whales are also called Orcas," he added. "And they're divided into three ecotypes. Do you remember what they are?"

My father was a wonderful teacher. Over the past two years, he had taught me all about whales and dolphins.

"I think so," I answered. "Residents are the ones that stay in the same area. Uh, offshores are the ones that are offshore and don't come too close in. And...I forget the last one."

He gave me a patient smile. "Transients. They're the ones that move around a lot. Some have even been sighted miles away from their original location. They're a bit unpredictable and often eat other mammals."

"Well, Professor Richardson, are you ready for dessert?" my mother said with a laugh as she reached for his plate.

His hand shot out and grabbed hers. With a shriek, she jumped back. My father stared at her, then kissed her fingers.

"I thought that *was* dessert," he teased, his eyes wide with feigned innocence.

"Yeah, but you never know where my fingers have been, Jack." She snatched her hand back and pretended to pick her nose.

"Ew!" I groaned.

My parents started laughing and it was contagious. Soon I joined them. Every time my mother snorted, we'd break into another fit of laughter.

Sometimes my family was so weird.

My mother and father were always touching each other, holding hands and kissing like teenagers. Most of the time I quite liked it. But sometimes when my friends were around, I found it rather embarrassing.

"What are you doing tomorrow?" my father asked me.

I told him about my plans to meet Goldie again on the beach.

He asked my mother the same question.

"I'm not telling," she said, smiling mysteriously.

I went up to my room after supper and wrote a long letter to Amber-Lynn. I gave her a detailed account of the trip to Bamfield. Then I described my new house and my big bay window. I told her about the raft and swimming in the ocean. I even told her about Robert. But I never mentioned a word about Goldie. I sensed that Amber-Lynn might feel jealous of my new friend, so I told her about my father's work, the new schooner and all about echolocation. I knew *that* would impress her.

When I finished writing the letter, I crawled into bed.

Sometime during the night, I had a dream that I was swimming in the ocean while a full moon ascended overhead. The water was warm and soothing, and I had no fear of it. As I floated on my back and looked up at the stars, restless waves gently nudged me back to shore.

Suddenly, a whisper of movement under the water caught my eye. A streak of black and white rushed by me, just under the surface.

A killer whale.

Its gleaming body shone in the opalescent glow of the moon.

I reached out a hand as it slid past me at a leisurely pace. Its smooth slippery skin was like the softest satin. It turned and swam past me again. Then the whale sank into the depths below.

After that, I slept peacefully.

I barely recalled that dream when I awoke the next morning, but many months later I remembered it and wondered if it was some kind of omen.

I know now that it was.

I met Goldie every afternoon in July and we became fast friends and confidants. She had a keen sense of adventure and a great imagination. She loved to tell me stories of her ancestors—legends from ancient times—and I was fascinated by them. From those stories, I learned to appreciate nature and the animals around me. We often saw bald eagles soaring overhead, and sometimes white-tailed deer would wander out from the forest.

One afternoon, she invited me to her house to meet her grandmother. "Everyone says Nana is special. You'll love her."

Nana was a wrinkled wise woman with the strangest hair I had ever seen. It hung down past her waist, thick and blacker than coal—except for one piece that framed the left side of her face. It was pure white.

She had deep amber-colored eyes that always sparkled. And like a hawk, she never missed anything. She seemed to know things—things that no human should know.

The first time I saw her, she was sitting in a rocking chair with her back to the door. She didn't even flinch when we walked inside. I thought that maybe she was sleeping.

"Nana," Goldie said. "This is—"

"Your friend Sarah," Nana finished without turning around.

Casting the old woman a nervous look, I sat down at the table. Goldie passed me a plate of oatmeal cookies and I took one.

"Take another one," Nana said behind me.

I peeked over my shoulder. She still wasn't facing us.

How did she know?

Without warning, Nana looked at me and smiled. "Eat. You're too skinny. I can always make more."

The rest of that afternoon, I felt her eyes burning into the back of my head. They seemed to follow me everywhere I went.

"Told you you'd love her," Goldie said under her breath.

I didn't have the heart to tell her the truth. I thought Nana was a bit spooky.

"Hey," my new friend said later. "I'll walk you home."

As we strolled along the shore, she told me that Nana was a respected healer. Almost everyone in Bamfield went to her for natural homeopathic remedies. She was knowledgeable about every plant that grew on the island and she could heal cuts and bruises with a few leaves from her garden. Every morning, she made special teas from tree bark and other ingredients that induced sleep or calmed the nerves.

"And she has a special gift," Goldie said mysteriously.

"What?" I asked.

She told me that sometimes Nana would simply look at someone and prescribe them a special remedy—before *they* even knew they were sick.

"That's because she sees auras," Goldie said.

She explained to me that auras were colored lights that her grandmother saw around someone's head or body. Few people saw those lights. Only those with *'the gift'*.

Nana was a wise woman—in more ways than I realized.

The following weekend, Goldie invited me to stay for a sleepover. We raced back to my place to get permission from my parents. Then we collected my pajamas, toothbrush and some games.

Back at her house, we unrolled sleeping bags in the loft overlooking the living room. The ceiling was slanted and we had to duck in some areas. Once, I forgot and walked straight into the beam. Goldie spent the rest of the night yelling *"Duck!"* every time I stood up.

That night, we munched on homemade trail mix and buttery popcorn. We told stories and giggled long into the night—until Goldie's mom yelled at us to go to sleep.

The Dixons were very nice, even when we kept them up until the wee hours of the morning. Mr. Dixon was a commercial fisherman and was often out on his fishing boat. Mrs. Dixon wove beautiful baskets with pictures of animals on them. She sold her baskets in a charming craft shop in town.

Every morning, they left Goldie and her sister Shonda with Nana for most of the day. Shonda was a quiet child. We rarely ever saw her. She spent most of the time with Nana, helping her in the kitchen. The Dixon house always smelled like fresh-baked cookies and warm bread and Nana often gave me treats to take home to my mother.

One day, she taught me how to make bannock—fried bread served warm and dripping with butter and honey. I made a perfect batch, according to her.

"Are you sure you aren't Indian?" she teased in her raspy voice.

She would often comment on my dark coloring and my love for nature. She said that I was part Indian, but that I just didn't know which part yet.

I think she made it her duty to help me find it.

Usually when I slept over, we'd have a bonfire outside. We'd sit around the crackling fire and roast hotdogs and marshmallows on sharpened sticks.

Nana would tell us incredible stories. Sometimes, she'd even act them out. I loved listening to her—especially her old Nootka legends. She would mesmerize us with the adventures of Eagle or Bear. She would scare us with stories of strange and fierce creatures.

Then one night, she told us the legend of Sisiutl.

four

"Sisiutl was a great sea monster," Nana said in her raspy voice. "It roamed the land and sea of the Nootka and Kwakiutl peoples. The monster was huge and ugly, with two great heads. And it could change into different shapes and sizes. Sisiutl could disguise itself, so it could prey upon unsuspecting animals or humans. It was believed that anyone who looked upon this great monster would be turned to stone."

She turned her back to us for a moment. When she whipped her head around and roared, I shrieked, toppling backward over the log that I was sitting on.

"It's a mask," Goldie said with a giggle as she helped me up.

I stared at Nana, horrified.

Her wrinkled face had been transformed into a terrifying, grotesque creature. The mask was made of wood and painted in dark, bright colors. Spiked black hair sprung from the top, and it had long earlobes and tattoos on its face. But it was the mask's expression that frightened me most. The creature's eyes bulged, its mouth a huge gaping hole. A permanent scream.

"My great, great grandfather once knew a man who met with this monster," Nana said, her voice muffled by the mask. "His body is still frozen in stone, somewhere in the mountains."

She hobbled over to a huckleberry bush and picked a handful of the tiny red berries. She crushed them between her hands.

"It is believed that if a warrior could injure Sisiutl and take some of the monster's blood and rub it on his skin, the blood would make the warrior's skin so strong that no enemy's weapons could pierce it." She rubbed the juice on my arm. "So many warriors tried in vain to get some of Sisiutl's blood. And so many men died trying." She removed the mask and looked at me with kind, caring eyes. "Great warriors never stop trying."

With her strange hair and knowing eyes, Nana made us believe almost anything. She would often watch me during her storytelling and sometimes I

23

wondered if she was trying to tell me something.

Now I know she was.

One morning in August, I was surprised to find my mother waiting for me outside on the deck. On the picnic table beside her was a basket filled with fruit and muffins that she had made the night before.

"I've decided to come with you today," she announced. "To meet Goldie's grandmother."

Nana had been asking about my mother and I desperately wanted them to meet. My parents had already met Goldie. My mother liked her so much that she often asked my friend if she wanted to stay for a sleepover. Goldie never refused. And she never said no to dinner at my house either. She loved my mother's Italian cooking.

I pointed at the basket. "Is that for Nana?"

"I wanted to bring her something," my mother said, chewing her bottom lip thoughtfully. "But I don't know if she likes lemon muffins. What do you think, Sarah?"

"I think she'll love them."

We set off down the path and followed the beach around the bend. We passed the boat dock where a small outboard was moored, then the Dixon's house came into view. The house seemed unusually silent, almost abandoned. Outside, some of Shonda's toys were scattered in the grass and a half-woven basket sat on a table next to a lawn chair. Hanging from a tree, a wind chime tinkled merrily in the soft breeze.

I knocked on the door. "Is anyone here?"

No answer.

I stepped inside.

"Sarah," my mother admonished.

"They told me to walk right in," I said. "Sometimes they go for walks in the woods."

I looked around the room. On the floor near the rocking chair sat a laundry basket. It was piled high with freshly laundered clothes, a few folded shirts nearby. In the kitchen, something fragrant was brewing in a pot on top of the stove.

"Goldie!" I yelled. "Where are you?"

My mother flinched at the sound of my loud voice.

"Their door is never closed to friends," I said, grinning. "Nana told me that. Can we wait for them?"

"I guess so."

It was obvious that she was more than a little uncomfortable about walking into a stranger's home before being invited in.

"It's an interesting house," she said, admiring the colorful Indian artwork and black argillite carvings.

The Dixon house was made of cedar, inside and out. It was small compared to our house. There were three bedrooms upstairs. Goldie's parents had the largest one, Goldie and Shonda shared a room and then there was Nana's. There was also the small loft area just off the upper hall, where Goldie and I slept when I came over for a sleepover.

The furniture in the living room on the lower floor was old and worn, but very comfortable. A large woven rug in rich amber and forest-green tones covered most of the floor between the couch and the fireplace. There was a simple kitchen with a table and six chairs crammed into one corner. Copper pots and pans decorated the kitchen walls and bunches of freshly picked herbs wrapped with twine hung on hooks to dry.

"I'm sure they'll be back soon," I said anxiously.

My mother glanced at her watch. "We'll wait just a few more minutes."

We sat down at the kitchen table and I stared at the clock on the wall.

Ten minutes passed. Then we heard voices and footsteps.

"Sarah?" Nana called from outside. "Are you in there, child?"

Goldie, Shonda and Nana stepped inside.

"How'd you know it was me?" I asked Goldie's grandmother.

The old woman winked. "The birds told me."

My mother smiled and reached out a hand. "I'm Sarah's mother. Daniella Richardson."

Nana did something that shocked me. She brushed away my mother's offered hand and engulfed her in a hug. My mother didn't quite know what to do.

I hid my face so that I wouldn't burst out laughing.

What an odd sight they made—my tall, slim mother gripped in a bear hug by a short, plump Indian woman.

"Call me Nana," the old woman said. "Everyone does. I'm so glad you came to visit me." She smiled. "Daniella. That's a very pretty name."

"Thank you," my mother replied.

Goldie tugged at my hand. "Let's go down to the beach."

I looked over my shoulder and saw Nana opening the basket my mother had brought. She pulled out a lemon muffin and bit into it hungrily while they chatted about our move to Canada. Watching the two women, I was happy that my mother had someone she could talk to. I knew that she missed her parents who were vacationing in Italy.

We brought Shonda with us down to the beach and watched the little girl play in the sand at the water's edge. She found some baby crabs in a small pool of water and brought them over to show us. She was a happy child with big black eyes. Sometimes she would gaze across the bay and I wondered if she was thinking of her brother.

"Do you miss Robert?" I asked Goldie.

She nodded and stared out toward Fallen Island. "I miss his laughter the most. He was always telling funny jokes. And playing pranks on Nana. One time he hid her herbs and when she went to hang them in the kitchen, she thought she'd never picked them at all. So she went back into the garden and cut some more."

"What did Robert do?"

"He hid those too," she replied with a wide grin. "When Nana went to hang the second bunch, she thought she was losing her mind because she couldn't find them either. She walked around the house muttering *'Now where did I put those darn herbs? I picked them, didn't I?'* It was hilarious."

I laughed at her impression of her grandmother.

"What was Robert doing?" I asked.

"He pretended he was asleep on the couch. But when Nana went back out into the garden a third time, he burst out laughing."

"Did she catch him?"

Goldie nodded. "You should've seen her. She marched back into the house with two buckets full of herbs, caught him laughing and realized right away what he'd done. Then she put the buckets on the floor by the couch and the next thing he knew, Robert was being hauled up by his ear."

I giggled. "Was he grounded?"

"No, Nana had a better punishment. She made him sit down at the kitchen table, then gave him a ball of twine and some scissors. She told him he had to divide each kind of herb into three piles, tie them with twine and hang them. It was *so* funny."

"I bet he didn't think so."

"Well, first he complained. Said he didn't want to waste his time hanging *weeds*. Then Nana told him that the three piles represented the three times *she* wasted going out to the garden to pick them."

"Did he do it?"

"What do you think?" she asked wryly. "Can you imagine anyone not doing what Nana tells them to do?"

Her laughter was infectious. I giggled so hard my sides ached. And Goldie laughed until she looked like she was going to cry.

Suddenly, a branch snapped behind us.

We stifled our giggles and turned around.

"What are you laughing at?" my mother asked, stepping out from the trees.

26

Beside her stood Nana.

I gave her an innocent smile. "Nothing, Mom. Just girl stuff."

Goldie muffled a snicker beside me and I jabbed her.

"Your mother has invited me for tea," Nana said, her eyes strangely serious.

Goldie and I exchanged thrilled looks.

Then we watched her grandmother and my mother stroll side-by-side down the beach—Nana with her coal-black hair loose from its braid and my mother with her fiery auburn hair tied in a casual ponytail.

They were an intriguing, peculiar pair.

That summer two friendships were born. Goldie and I became the best of friends, seldom arguing about anything. And Nana and my mother exchanged visits a couple of times a week.

I knew that their friendship was real the day my mother invited Nana to enter her secret domain. In fact, Goldie's grandmother was the only person to see my mother's first Vancouver Island painting before it was even finished.

My mother was captivated by Nana's Nootka legends and the new painting was a tribute to them. It featured a magnificent gray wolf looking into a crystal pool of water while a young Indian girl's face stared back in the reflection. It was mystically beautiful and my mother refused to sell it. Instead, she made prints and sent them off to the gallery. The director of *Visions* requested more paintings with similar themes and I hardly saw my mother for the next two weeks, except for when she visited Nana.

During one of the last visits before school started, Nana prepared a delicious lunch of venison stew and biscuits. We ate outside under a towering forest of trees. We listened to the squawking seabirds and the restless waves crashing upon the shore.

Afterward, we picked huckleberries. My mother laughed when Shonda came back with a nearly empty bucket, her mouth reddened by berry juice.

That was the summer I became Indian—at least, in spirit.

Nana even gave me my own Indian name. *Hai Nai Yu.*

One evening, we sat around a huge bonfire and had a special naming ceremony. Nana sang strange words in her native tongue and brushed my face with an eagle's feather.

I was fascinated.

When I asked her where the name came from, she told me the legend of Copper Woman and Copper Woman's granddaughter, Hai Nai Yu.

"Copper Woman had been alive for many generations, her body still young to look upon. She felt tired and ready to move on, to do other things she could not do in human form. Hai Nai Yu went with her grandmother and learned about

27

wisdom and life."

Nana pulled a copper ring from her pocket and gave it to me.

"Copper Woman told Hai Nai Yu that wisdom must always be passed on to women, no matter what color their skin. Copper Woman told her granddaughter that all people come from the same blood. And blood is sacred." She gave me a handful of huckleberries.

"Hai Nai Yu promised to become the guardian of the wisdom and to share it when her time came. Then Copper Woman walked the beach alone and became Old Woman."

She tossed something into the fire and the fire flared.

"Her bones turned into a loom and a broom," she said.

I loved that story. And I adored Nana even more for giving me that extraordinary name.

Hai Nai Yu—The Wise One of the One Who Knows.

From that moment on, *Hai Nai Yu* was the only name she called me. I often wondered why she picked that particular name.

I sure didn't feel very wise back then.

five

School started the first week in September. Goldie had told me so much about some of the teachers that I felt I already knew them. We kept our fingers crossed, praying that we'd end up in the same grade six classroom. There were two rooms per grade, so we knew that the odds were in our favor. I couldn't wait for school to start.

Looking back now, I realize just how naïve I had been. I never had a clue of what was in store for me.

On the first morning, Goldie dropped by my house and we took the small yellow bus to school together.

"Want me to come with you?" my mother asked.

I was horrified. I was too old to have her bring me to school. I'd be teased mercilessly.

Goldie took my arm. "I'll take care of her, Mrs. Richardson."

We waved goodbye and hurried toward the bus.

During the entire drive to school, I stared out the window while Goldie chattered about all the field trips we'd go on. My stomach churned as I thought about a new classroom, new teachers and being the new kid.

I was more than a bit nervous.

"Please let us get the same classroom," I whispered.

Lady Luck was with us in the form of an old Indian woman with a white streak in her pitch-black hair. I found out later that Nana had spoken to the principal. She'd made sure that Goldie and I were placed in the same classroom.

I followed my friend through the arced doorway of the school and down the crowded hallway. I tried to walk inconspicuously, but my squeaking shoes betrayed me.

"We're over here," Goldie said with a giggle.

She steered me toward a windowless door at the end of the hall. We heard laugher and deafening voices coming from inside.

29

WHALE SONG

With a deep breath, I pushed open the door. A paper airplane spiraled toward me and I ducked. The boy who launched it grinned, his golden eyes gleaming mischievously.

"Move, Sarah," Goldie hissed, pushing me forward. "If we hurry, we might get to sit beside each other."

Two of the walls in the small classroom were covered with colorful posters and small windows. The other two walls held wall-sized blackboards. There were twenty-one students and twenty-two flip-top desks.

Goldie slid into a chair and stretched out her arm, saving me the seat across the aisle. Relieved, I sat down and emptied the contents of my backpack into the desk. Then I took out a pen and notebook and set them on top.

The teacher clapped her hands and called for attention. "We have a new student this year," she said, smiling.

I let out a groan, wishing that I could slide under my desk.

"Sarah Richardson has traveled here all the way from the United States," the teacher continued. "Sarah, can you please stand so we can welcome you properly?"

There was a tentative round of applause when I scrambled to my feet. My hand slipped and the notebook toppled to the floor. I picked it up—my face feverishly hot and my legs shaking. Then I dove for my chair.

"I'm Mrs. Higginson," the teacher said, writing her name on the blackboard. "Now class...shall we begin?"

Mrs. Higginson was a wonderful, plump woman who wore neatly pressed dresses and speckled glasses that dangled from a golden chain around her neck. She was originally from England and I loved her accent so much I often imitated it.

Most of the children in our school had lived on Vancouver Island all their lives. In my class, there were only four other kids who were not Indian. At first, I thought nothing of it. Some of my friends back in Wyoming were Shoshone. But it wasn't long before I learned about racism. And hatred.

On the second day of school, the class bully took out a pair of scissors and gave me an impromptu haircut. She sat behind me, so I didn't even feel it. I didn't know anything was wrong until she flung a handful of long hair on my desk after school.

One look at her short dark hair and I knew it wasn't hers.

I was mortified.

The classroom was empty. Mrs. Higginson was gone and Goldie had already headed to the boot room.

I stood there, gazing at the butchered hair on the desk while Annie Pierce, a stocky native girl, stared at me with a smug look on her face.

"Well?" she sneered. "Whatcha got to say, *white* girl?"

As tears welled in my eyes, I battled with my raging emotions and snatched up the pieces of hair.

What did I do to deserve this?

Annie grabbed my shirt with her fist. Her scowling mouth was so close to my nose that I thought she would bite it off.

"Say a word to anyone," she warned. "And I'll make you sorry you ever moved here."

She gave me a hard shove and stalked out of the room.

Mrs. Higginson returned a few minutes later and discovered me curled up in my chair.

"What's wrong, Sarah?" she asked in a kind voice.

I tried to hide my miserable tears and struggled with my options. *Should I tell her what happened—or keep quiet?*

In the end, I chose silence.

"Nothing, Mrs. Higginson," I said with a sniffle. "I'm fine."

I quickly gathered the pieces of my hair, hoping that she wouldn't see what I was doing. I hid my hands behind my back, walked over to the garbage can and deposited the hair. Then I grabbed my backpack and hurried out of the school.

"What took you so long?" Goldie asked when I caught up to her at the bus stop.

"Mrs. Higginson wanted to talk to me," I lied.

I didn't mention the haircutting episode with Annie because I wasn't sure if they were friends or not.

On the bus, I was quiet.

"What's wrong?" Goldie asked me.

"I'm just tired."

When the bus reached my house, I hurried down the steps, waved goodbye and rushed inside my house. I hung my jacket in the closet and called out for my mother.

"I'm upstairs!" she yelled back. "I'm almost done painting for today. Be down in a bit, okay?"

Minutes later, she trotted downstairs and joined me on the deck where I was drinking chocolate milk.

"How was school?" she asked.

"It was…okay," I said hesitantly. "Can you cut my hair?"

Her face registered her shock. "Why on earth would you want to cut your hair? It's beautiful the way it is. And you know your father likes it long."

"I know," I mumbled. "I just want…a change. Can you cut it to the top of my shoulders?"

After supper—much to my father's dismay—my mother dug out her scissors and comb. When she found the section that Annie had already attacked, she paused and I held my breath.

"What happened here, Sarah?"

"I, uh, tried to cut it myself," I said quickly.

She resumed cutting. "Well next time just ask me. Don't try to do it yourself. You made a mess back here."

Yeah, I made a mess of something.

I thought about Annie. Obviously I had said or done something to offend her. But I couldn't think of what that was. I had barely spoken two words to her.

"There," my mother said, brushing my hair. "All done."

I ran upstairs to my room and looked in the dresser mirror. I swung my head from side-to-side, admiring myself, pleased to discover that my new hairstyle actually suited me. My brown hair was streaked with copper by the summer sun and a natural wave had bounced back because of all the layering my mother had done.

I smiled. "Not bad."

I had no idea the attention I'd receive the next day, but I did know one thing. Annie had done me a favor.

The next morning, I plodded up the steps of the bus and made my way to the seat beside Goldie. When she caught sight of my new hairstyle, she gasped.

Then she grinned. "It looks good. But why'd you cut it?"

I shrugged. "Annie Pierce gave me the idea."

She frowned. "What do you mean?"

When I told her what Annie had done, Goldie's eyes grew dark and stormy. Part of me was nervous about what she might do, but the other part was thrilled at having such a loyal friend.

As we stepped off the bus, I noticed that Annie—with her short uncombed hair and mean eyes—was huddled in one corner with a small group of friends. I drew in an uneasy breath, but was surprised when she paid no attention to me at all.

I don't think she recognized me at first.

But once she did, her dark eyes flared with surprise. Then they narrowed in anger. She didn't say a word to me when Goldie and I walked by. My friend's furious expression, I think, told her enough.

I entered the classroom and Mrs. Higginson complimented me on my new style. I didn't know until much later that she had discovered the pieces of my hair in the garbage can. Or that she had found Annie's scissors.

When the day was over and the last bell rang, I grabbed my books and followed Goldie to the door.

"Sarah and Annie," Mrs. Higginson called. "Stay behind please."

I exchanged a worried look with Goldie who glared at Annie before disappearing into the hall. Reluctantly, I trudged toward Mrs. Higginson's desk. She was busy straightening papers and that made me more edgy.

"How has your first few days been, Sarah?" She glanced up and smiled at me, her eyes softening.

I looked from her to Annie. "Uh...good, I guess."

"Any problems?"

Annie heaved a sigh of impatience. "Why do I have to stay behind? I haven't done nothin'."

Mrs. Higginson's head whipped up. "Haven't you?"

She reached into her desk and pulled out a pair of blue-handled scissors—*Annie's* scissors. A few long brown hairs were still trapped between the blades.

She waved the scissors under Annie's nose. "What exactly *were* you cutting?"

Annie jabbed her elbow into my ribs and hissed under her breath. *"Don't say anything."*

"Sarah, do you want to tell me?" Mrs. Higginson asked, pursing her lips.

I shook my head. "No, it's okay."

She crossed her arms and stared at us for a few minutes. Then she looked at me and smiled. "By the way, your hair looks lovely. Don't you think so, Annie?"

The girl beside me remained mute—except for her enraged eyes. They flashed a message, loud and clear.

"Go on home, you two," Mrs. Higginson said with a sigh of quiet resignation. "And I don't want any more problems...Annie."

She escorted us to the classroom door and watched as we walked down the hall together. At the main school doors, I looked back over my shoulder. She was gone.

Scurrying down the steps, I veered off to the left, but Annie grabbed my arm.

"Better watch your back, white girl."

Petrified, I ran off to meet Goldie at the bus stop. We boarded the bus and it ambled off down the road, passing Annie along the way. She stared up at me as she walked alongside the ditch. She mouthed one word.

Bitch.

During my first week at Bamfield Elementary, the burden of being a *'white kid'* was almost too much to endure. Someone had poured glue into my desk, smeared mud on my jacket and one of my art projects had mysteriously disappeared.

Of course, only one person I knew would do those things.

On Thursday morning, I found a chocolate bar in my desk. I glanced around the classroom and tried to determine who had put it there. I was sure it had been Goldie.

Later, we sat outside in the grass and I showed her the treat.

"I found it in my desk."

Goldie gave a quick shrug. "Mrs. Higginson must've left it for you—seeing as you're teacher's pet." She grinned at me.

I peered over my shoulder and saw our teacher sitting on the steps. She smiled at me and waved.

"You must be right," I said, peeling back the wrapper from the chocolate bar. "Wanna bite?"

She eyed it hungrily. "You first. It's your chocolate bar."

I bit into the chewy treat, savoring the delicious flavor. Then I offered it to her. She laughed and grabbed it out of my hand. As she opened her mouth to take a bite, she gagged. Her horrified expression made me swallow what was already in my mouth.

It didn't go down easily.

Goldie moaned. "Ew, gross."

six

She held out the chocolate bar and pointed to a small hole in the wrapper. Inside, a wriggling mass of tiny bugs infested the bar. And I had eaten some of them.

My stomach heaved.

I spit out everything while Goldie tried to comfort me.

"Who would do such a thing?" she demanded.

Both of us knew the answer to that question.

We spun on our heels as Annie and her gang gathered behind us. All I could see were boys and girls laughing at me, calling me malicious names.

"The *white* girl eats bugs!" Annie screeched at the top of her lungs. "Don'tcher parents feed you real food?"

I cringed and wiped chocolate bug drool from the corner of my mouth. Determined not to cry, I blinked back hot tears.

Goldie jumped to her feet, hands on hips. "Annie, you oughta be ashamed," she shouted, furious. "That was a mean and nasty thing to do."

Annie let out a smug grunt. "Goldie, you goin' white? Don't you be gettin' better than us." Her eyes squinted dangerously.

I glanced up at my friend. Goldie looked like she was ready to pounce. Her eyes fired daggers. Even I was a bit afraid of her at that moment.

"Don't," I mumbled.

"That girl needs to be taught a lesson," she said through gritted teeth.

"This isn't your fight."

We watched Annie and her followers disperse into the school. Then we made our way toward the building, not knowing what to say to each other. I knew that Goldie was seething inside and plotting revenge against Annie. But my mind was on something else.

Were those bugs squirming around—alive—inside me?

I hugged my stomach and retched into some bushes near the steps. My eyes

35

streamed and I couldn't control the tears as they poured down my cheeks.

Goldie, my steadfast friend, rubbed my back and handed me a napkin. "You okay?"

I sniffed and nodded.

When the school bell rang after lunch, I steeled myself, wiped my face with my sleeve and went inside. I sat at my desk, refusing to look behind me or even acknowledge Annie. I felt her burning stare all day—a day that passed so slowly I thought I'd die from humiliation or fear.

Goldie was unusually quiet that afternoon. She barely said a word—even to me. I caught her glaring at Annie a few times and I knew that I was lucky to have such a loyal friend.

The following morning when everyone arrived at school, we were greeted with an unusual sight. Halfway up the flagpole, someone had strung up a pair of shabby floral shorts and a small white bra. They flapped in the brisk fall breeze.

I nudged Goldie. "I wonder who those belong to."

"Yeah," my friend said innocently. "I wonder."

Bobbie Livingston, a blonde-haired boy from the other sixth grade classroom, nudged the boy next to him. I had been admiring the second boy from a distance for days.

Adam Reid.

Goldie had once told me that Adam's mother was native, but that his father was white. That explained Adam's permanent tan.

He was a few months older than I was, tall, athletic and very popular. He had a mop of wavy hair, the most unusual golden eyes and the cutest lopsided smile. When he grinned at me that first day after he'd thrown the paper airplane my way, I thought I had died and gone to heaven. At eleven years old, I was already half in love with him.

"I think those are Annie's," Adam said. "That bra's kinda small though."

A wave of laughter washed over the crowd.

At that moment, Annie stormed across the field and pushed her way through to the flagpole. "Hey! What's going on? What are you—?"

"That your *brassiere*?" Bobbie asked with a snicker.

Annie turned slowly, her face a mix of disbelief and dread. When she looked up and saw her shorts and bra on the pole, her entire body went still and her face blazed with heat.

The surrounding laughter dimmed to whispers.

Her mouth quivered. "Who the hell—?" She spun around, her enraged eyes searching out the crowd.

She looked at me for a moment on me, but she frowned and shook her head.

She stared into each tense face until her black eyes settled on Goldie.

Stunned, I gazed at my friend. "You did it?"

Goldie threw me a sly smile. "What if I did?"

"You're gonna pay for this," Annie hissed. "You too, Sarah."

Goldie reached out and gripped my arm. It felt like she was branding me, warning the others that I wasn't to be touched. And it worked…for a while. After that, no one bothered me—except Annie. But that was later.

As we headed for the door, I stole a peek at Goldie.

I can't quite explain why, but amidst the whispers and laughter, I felt a deep sadness. She had stuck up for me—had even gotten revenge—while I had quivered in fear. In that moment, she became my new *best* friend. Amber-Lynn was in the past.

I walked up the steps, then glanced over my shoulder.

The field was almost empty. Only one person remained.

Annie.

She stood there—alone and disgraced. Her shoulders were slumped and I wasn't positive, but it looked like she was crying.

Turning away, I took a deep breath and went inside.

The entire school was called to an emergency assembly in the gym and the students of Bamfield Elementary were lectured about bullying and warned of the consequences.

The principal was furious. "Whoever's responsible for this disgraceful behavior should come forward now."

Thankfully, Goldie remained silent.

With an irritated huff, the principal eyed the room. "If any of you know who is responsible, you know where to find me. I expect a name by the end of the day." His expression darkened. "The culprit will be severely reprimanded."

For the rest of the day, I chewed my fingernails and anxiously waited for Goldie to be dragged out of class. I was sure she'd be sent home with a detention.

Strangely enough, nobody turned her in.

What surprised me most was that not even Annie mentioned Goldie's involvement, even though she'd been questioned for over half an hour. She returned to class later that day and passed by me without a second glance.

Part of me felt sorry for Annie.

Part of me feared what she would do next.

The day passed uneventfully. After school, Goldie and I raced to the crowded bus stop to wait for the bus. As it groaned to a halt in front of us, I pulled her aside.

"*Was* it you?" I whispered.

Her eyes caught mine. "Does it really matter who did it?"

WHALE SONG

I was silent for a moment.

"No. It doesn't matter at all."

We climbed aboard the bus, sat down in our usual seats and hardly said a word to each other during the ride home. When the bus reached the entrance to my driveway, I mumbled a quick goodbye and hopped down the steps. The road to my house seemed never-ending and I trudged along, dragging my feet in the sand and gravel.

That's when I realized something.

I was ashamed of what Goldie had done to Annie on my behalf. I was mortified that I was the cause of someone's public humiliation. The guilt ate at me.

Until I remembered the bug-infested chocolate bar.

Then the rage set in.

"You're awfully quiet tonight," my father said during supper. "What's up, Sarah?"

Pushing my cold mashed potatoes to one side of my plate, I looked at him. My eyes burned with the need to tell him how much I hated living in Bamfield, how much I hated school and how mean everyone was—everyone except Goldie. I yearned to tell him about Annie and the horrible things that she had done to me.

I opened my mouth to speak. But nothing came out.

"Sarah?" my father repeated. "Are you—?"

"Can I be excused, Dad? I don't feel so good."

"Of course."

The words were scarcely out of his mouth when I jumped to my feet and rushed upstairs to my room. Closing the bedroom door behind me, I threw myself down on my bed.

"I hate it here," I sobbed. "And I hate Annie."

I grabbed my pillow and flung it against the door. My face was wet and my throat felt like a fiery furnace. It was hard to be quiet when what I really wanted to do was bawl and scream.

I thought of Annie and my blood boiled. How would I survive three years of being the *white kid*? How would I endure the malevolent spitefulness of Annie Pierce?

My hatred of her was so intense that I longed to lash out at her, to hurt her physically. I envisioned revenge. My *own* sweet revenge. I couldn't allow Goldie to be my savior forever, to be there for me every time Annie decided to be cruel. I needed to be strong, to defend myself. I wanted to overcome my fear of her. I just didn't know how.

I curled up on my bed, depressed and angry, plotting all the vengeful things

I would do to Annie. I don't know how much time passed before there was a soft knock on the door.

"Sarah?"

The bed sagged as my mother sat on the edge of the mattress.

"Are you okay, honey?"

Her voice cracked a bit and I sensed her sadness.

"Do you want to talk about it?"

I shook my head.

She stretched out beside me and we lay side-by-side, shoulders touching. We stayed like that for a long time, neither of us saying a word.

Working up my nerve, I said, "There's this girl at school. Annie. She's the one who cut my hair. And she gave me a chocolate bar with bugs in it." I took a deep breath and looked at my mother. "Everyone teased me and Annie called me *white girl*."

My mother was appalled. "That's horrible. I'll talk to your teacher."

I shook my head. "No! That'll make things worse."

"Annie must be a terribly sad and angry girl."

I stared at her, confused by her comment. How could my mother feel any sympathy toward the girl that was bullying me?

"What do you mean?" I asked in a sulky voice.

She patted my hand and entwined her elegant fingers through mine. "Usually when kids act like that toward someone else, it's because *they* are unhappy. Annie may be jealous of you. Or maybe a white person treated her badly at one time and that's why she seems to hate white people."

I opened my mouth to argue, but she cut me off. "That's called racism, Sarah. When you judge someone or dislike them for the color of their skin or their race. When Nonno Rocco and Nonna Sophia first came to North America, many people were mean to them because they were Italian. People can be spiteful sometimes—especially children. Some people just don't know any better. No one's taught them that it's wrong to judge others by the color of their skin."

I pouted. "Why didn't Annie's parents teach her it's wrong?"

She gave a sad shrug. "I don't know, honey. Sometimes kids learn from their parents how to hate other people. I really don't know why Annie feels the way she does."

I clenched her hand, wondering how she could always see something good in everyone, no matter how nasty they were. That was why my mother was so special.

But I wasn't like her. I *hated* Annie.

The bed shifted as my mother rose to her feet. "What are you going to do, Sarah?"

39

I moaned. "I don't know, Mom. What *can* I do?"

"Hating Annie will suck out your own goodness and energy. You're so much better than that. If you choose to hate her, then you become just like her—no better." She kissed my forehead and hugged me. "Life's too short to not forgive those who hurt us. I trust you to do what's right. Right by your own heart." She placed her palm against my beating heart. "Forgiveness sets you free."

Outside the bay window, the sky was woven with fiery cumulus clouds and the sun drifted below the trees. A bald eagle dipped low, soared past the window and disappeared into the night.

As I went to sleep, the last thing I thought of was my mother's parting words.

"Forgiveness sets you free."

seven

Two days passed by without any repercussions from Annie.

Throughout the week, I kept my mother's advice close to heart, trying to find a way to forgive the girl. But forgiveness didn't come easily to me. I eventually gave up my ideas of revenge when I noticed that even Annie's friends were ostracizing her. I figured that was punishment enough.

When she showed up at school on Wednesday with a black eye, I almost felt sorry for her. She told Mrs. Higginson that she'd been hit by a ball at the park. Goldie and I suspected that she'd run into someone's fist. Wishful thinking on our part.

That night, my father bounded into the house. He had a huge smile on his face.

"Guess what? Jeff Boyd, the research coordinator, just announced that the new schooner, complete with the best echolocation equipment, will be arriving tomorrow." He pulled my mother close and grinned like a circus clown.

"Will you get to drive it?" I asked, bouncing on my chair.

He chuckled. "No, there'll be a real skipper doing the driving. My job is to monitor the electronic sound equipment. I'll be out in the schooner for the next two months." His eyes gleamed suddenly. "Sarah, do you think your class would be interested in a field trip aboard the *Finland Fancy* on Friday?"

"Really? You'll take us all out?"

In my imagination, I was already on that boat.

My mother smiled. "That's a wonderful idea, Jack."

There was such excitement in the air as he picked my mother off the ground and spun her around in his arms. She laughed breathlessly and batted at him with both hands.

"Jack!" she shrieked. "Put me down!"

His eyes held a wicked twinkle. "And what if I don't?"

"You're making me dizzy," she warned.

41

He set her down and she stumbled against the table.

"See?" she chastised him. "If I walk into a wall, it's your fault."

I forgot all about my mother's clumsiness as we celebrated the arrival of the schooner and my father's new job. My parents' happiness was infectious. We rode a wave of joy that night and all my problems seemed to have disappeared.

But even I should have known that things would change.

After all…all good things must come to an end.

On Friday morning, I bolted out of bed, dressed hurriedly and raced downstairs. I couldn't shut up about the field trip that my father had arranged with the principal and Mrs. Higginson. It was set for ten that morning.

"Finland Fancy field trip," I announced.

My mother grinned. "Fun and fabulous Finland Fancy field trip."

I sang that phrase repeatedly, fascinated by the tongue twister effect. I think my parents were relieved when I headed to school.

After a boring lecture on boat safety, Mrs. Higginson corralled us toward the bus and we piled in, chattering in youthful anticipation. We endured a bumpy bus ride to the harbor and then raced down to the dock where the *Finland Fancy* was anchored.

My gaze swept across the names on the boats. "Where is it?"

Goldie's smile drooped. "Over there."

As soon as I saw the boat, my heart immediately sank.

The research schooner was in rough shape. Its neglected hull was a battered white and needed painting. The trim was pine green and the cedar deck was weathered and uneven.

"I thought you said the *Finland Fancy* was new," I complained as my father helped me onto the boat.

"Well, it's new for us. It just needs some sprucing up, maybe some fresh paint."

"Or a sledgehammer," I mumbled without missing a beat.

He laughed. "Come on. She's not that bad. And she's fast."

I wasn't impressed. I had spent the last few days telling everyone how great the boat was going to be, that it had come all the way from Finland…that it was new.

"Hope this thing doesn't sink," I said dryly.

"Me too," the skipper said behind me.

Skip, as he was known, was a weathered-faced jovial seaman with snow-white hair and a bushy beard. Because he puffed on a sweet-smelling tobacco pipe, I wanted to call him *Captain High Liner*, after the frozen fish my mother liked to buy. But I never worked up enough nerve.

"Welcome aboard," he said. "I'm your skipper for today's adventure aboard the *Titanic*." He grinned at me. "I mean, the *Finland Fancy*."

Nervous laughter trickled from my classmates while I suspiciously eyed the boat.

Goldie elbowed me. "I hope we don't hit an iceberg."

"Or an ice cube," I muttered.

Mrs. Higginson seemed a little *'green at the gills'*, as my father put it later. She gingerly gathered the folds of her denim skirt and stepped onto the twenty-foot research schooner. The kids in my class filed on board behind her. Some appeared quite nervous, but they were all impressed by the boat—and by my father.

Skip directed us to deck chairs and bench seats, and Goldie and I were just settling down beside each other when Bobbie, who was sitting across from us, snorted loudly.

"Jeez, would ya look at Annie," he said.

Heads swiveled in unison and we all gaped as Annie awkwardly climbed aboard the schooner. All eyes were drawn to her left arm and there was a collective gasp of shock. Annie had a broken arm. And it was wrapped in a cast and sling.

Mrs. Higginson rushed to her side. "What happened, dear?"

Annie shrugged. "I fell off my bike."

Goldie and I watched in disbelief as our teacher fussed over and pampered my archenemy. Annie sat down on a deck chair and let out a soft whimper. The sound sent Mrs. Higginson scurrying for a pillow.

"Think she's faking?" I asked Goldie.

"Naw, the cast is real."

"I don't think she fell off her bike. I think she got into a fight."

Goldie snickered. "I wonder what the other guy looks like."

I couldn't resist a grin—until I glanced at Annie and caught her eye. She looked away too quickly and I knew that something wasn't right.

The schooner pulled away from the harbor and I quickly forgot all about her. Holding onto the rail, I stood beside my best friend and watched the houses grow smaller. The ocean became more restless the farther out we went and the schooner bobbed up and down in rhythm. Rays of light bounced off the metal equipment as the sun beamed across the deck.

Some of my classmates had never seen the ocean in such a way. Many had never even been on a boat. I thought that was odd, considering they lived on an island surrounded by water.

"Okay class," Mrs. Higginson called. "Move a bit closer to Professor Richardson."

"Does anyone know what this is?" my father asked.

He held up a small black object. It had a long cord that was attached to a forbidding piece of equipment with various colored knobs.

"A microphone," Adam answered promptly.

My father nodded. "But this is a special microphone. It's designed to go underwater, to pick up sounds that sea creatures make."

"Can we hear them?" Goldie asked.

"Once we're out far enough you can listen with a pair of headphones. That's what I do when I don't want any distractions. Or I can turn up the volume and we can all listen at the same time." He pointed to a large black knob.

He spent the next half-hour answering numerous questions, especially from the boys in my class. Adam appeared very interested in my father's work. He was glued to his side for the entire day. I think that was one of the happiest days for my father. His work captured all of our hearts that afternoon, and he handled a barrage of questions and kept all of us kids in line. I was so proud to be his daughter.

When Skip shut off the engines, all we heard was the sound of waves rippling against the boat. Before us, the ocean was endless, and its beauty and power captured us.

"The water is calmer out here," my father said. "In a few minutes we'll drop the microphone overboard."

"What sounds can you hear with it?" Mrs. Higginson asked, propping up her sunglasses with a chubby finger.

"You can hear almost any sea creature with this. Especially ones that use echolocation, such as whales, dolphins, seals, sea lions and many species of fish."

He reached over the side, unhooked the microphone and tossed it out into the ocean. Then he cranked up the volume and motioned us to wait.

Minutes went by. Nothing. Not a sound.

Then we heard a soft chirping noise.

"What's that?" Adam asked.

"Fish," my father said, smiling. "Halibut."

While we listened and waited, I stared out over the sea. Foamy waves dotted the horizon and pieces of deadwood floated around us.

I sighed impatiently. "I want to see killer whales."

Goldie nodded, her eyes searching the surface of the water. I knew that she was looking for telltale evidence of a whale pod. Or maybe her brother.

"I don't see anything," she said, disappointed.

My father sat next to the equipment, made some adjustments and listened with the headphones. Minutes later, he grinned, yanked off the headphones and handed them to the nearest child—Adam Reid, of course.

Adam's eyes lit up and I wondered what he was listening to that had him smiling so much. As soon as he removed the headphones, my father unplugged them and cranked up the speakers so we all could hear the strange sounds coming from below.

I shut my eyes and listened.

Something made a rapid clicking noise. Then I heard an eerie, forlorn wail. It reminded me of a baby crying for its mother. I heard it again, and a shiver tingled up and down my spine.

After a moment, I opened my eyes and looked at Goldie.

Her face was beaming.

"That's a killer whale," my father said. "In fact, it's a pod—a family. And they're coming closer."

The clicking sounds grew more agitated—like hundreds of agitated voices—and I held my breath in anticipation, my eyes glued to the water.

"Keep a lookout," my father warned, throwing me a quick wink.

All of a sudden, about twenty yards out, a spray of water shot into the air. Before my father could explain that a whale was spouting, a killer whale broke the surface. Its body was huge and sleek. It was the most splendid sight I'd ever seen.

"It's beautiful," I murmured.

The whale dove underwater and disappeared. A few seconds later, three whales emerged. And they headed straight for our boat.

"Oh no," Mrs. Higginson moaned. "They're going to hit us."

"No they're not," my father said, patting her arm. "They'll dive under. They're much farther away than they appear."

Some of the kids—including Goldie—nervously waited for the boat to sink. But I had faith in my father.

"Don't worry," I told my teacher. "If my dad says they'll dive under, then that's just what they'll do."

No sooner were the words out of my mouth, the whales sunk below the surface and reappeared a great distance behind us.

We ate lunch on the *Finland Fancy*, surrounded by a mystifying symphony of sea creatures. The schooner bobbed amongst pods of whales, a couple of dolphins and a curious sea lion. In the afternoon, we took out our binders and noted things of interest—until Mrs. Higginson announced a surprise quiz. It was conducted by my father who ignored our rolling eyes and proceeded to drill us on everything he had taught us that day.

For the last hour, Goldie slipped the headphones over her ears. She seemed just as captivated as I was by the immense beauty of the whales. A couple of times, I saw her nodding, as if in agreement to something she'd heard. Once, I noticed her lips moving and a radiant smile spread across her face. It was as if she had heard her brother's voice.

"Okay kids," my father said. "It's time to call it a day."

Amidst groans of disappointment, he turned off the sound equipment and raised the microphone. Then the *Finland Fancy* chugged back toward the harbor.

Once we were docked, my father pulled me aside. "Did you have a good time?"

"It was great," I said, grinning. "It's too bad Mom couldn't have come out with us."

"Maybe next time. She had a painting to finish for the gallery by Monday." He kissed my cheek. "I'll meet you at home and we'll see how she's doing with it."

During the bus ride back to school, Goldie and I compared notes about the day. Her eyes drifted shut, so I settled into my seat and closed my eyes too. I thought she was dozing, until I heard her snickering under her breath.

I eyed her suspiciously. "What?"

"Adam likes you, Sarah."

My face felt like it was on fire. "What do you mean?"

"He told Bobbie Livingston he thinks you're *cute*. Bobbie's sister Mary told Melanie and *she* told me."

I slunk low in my seat.

"Naw, I don't think anyone else knows," she said, reading my mind.

We turned and spied on Adam over the back of the seat. He was busy talking to Bobbie, so he didn't notice us.

I let out a dreamy sigh. "He *is* cute."

Suddenly, Adam turned his charismatic smile on me.

I froze. Then I dropped down into my seat.

Goldie leaned close. "What are you thinking?"

"I don't know."

It was just the smallest of white lies.

I gazed out the window, thinking that Adam was God's gift to young girls. And I couldn't imagine why he would like *me*. But I was glad that he did.

In a dazed, euphoric fog, I practically skipped into my house and headed upstairs.

"Mom?" My voice echoed in the silence. "Mom, are you up here?"

I checked her studio, but my mother wasn't there. Her painting sat unfinished and abandoned on the easel. I walked down the hall and knocked on her bedroom door. No answer.

I opened it anyway, expecting the room to be empty.

But it wasn't.

My mother was curled up in her bed, fast asleep. She didn't even stir when I approached her bedside.

"Mom?" I whispered.

She blinked. "Oh, you're home."

"Are you all right, Mom?"

"I'm fine, Sarah. Just tired."

Her voice was weary and her face seemed a bit pale as she brushed a hand across her forehead. That worried me. My mother was always full of energy.

"I'll let you go back to sleep," I murmured.

"No, come and sit down," she said, patting the bed. "How was the field trip?"

"It was great," I grinned. "Dad was great. We saw killer whales and seals…and you should've heard the sounds they made."

My mother yawned. "It sounds like you had a great time.

I looked down at her paint-splattered hands. "How come you didn't finish your painting?"

An odd look shadowed her face. "I'll finish it tomorrow. I just couldn't seem to stay awake today. Must be the ocean air." She pushed off the covers. "Hey, let's make supper."

"Okay. Can we have a barbecue?"

"That's a great idea." She stood up hastily and rubbed her legs. When she caught my worried look, she grinned. "That'll teach me for staying in bed all day. Now don't tell your father I was sleeping or I'll never hear the end of it."

"Sure," I said uneasily.

We ate grilled salmon steaks and potato salad outside on the deck. My father talked nonstop about the field trip. And about how impressed he was at some of the kids' questions during our field trip.

"That one boy…" he mused. "What was his name—Alan?"

"Adam," I corrected as the heat rose in my cheeks.

"Yes, that's it. Adam. He seemed very interested in my work. Asked lots of questions."

I crawled into bed, thinking of a tall, brown-haired boy with golden eyes. Did Adam really like me? I knew I liked him.

That night I dreamt of a pod of killer whales with golden eyes. They swam in the ocean depths, chattering to each other about their journey. How I longed to swim with them.

Over the weekend, I plodded through school projects and a heap of homework. The following Monday, I caught myself spying on Adam to see if he was even looking at me. By the end of the day, I was sure that someone had lied. He didn't seem to notice me from a hole in the ground.

I slumped into a depression.

An Indian summer blew in and warmed the sand and water. Each day after school, I walked along our little beach area and met up with Goldie. We swam out to the raft and my eyes were drawn toward Fallen Island. It almost seemed to call me and I was tempted to swim out to it. Until I remembered Goldie's brother.

And my promise to my father.

In late September, we took a family excursion on board the *Finland Fancy*. It was my mother's first time on a boat. Well, unless you counted the one-man pedal boat we used on our pond back in Wyoming.

As my mother crossed the deck and moved toward me, she grabbed the rail for support. "Can't you hold this thing still?"

My father laughed. "You need to get your sea legs, Dani."

He ruffled her hair and helped her to her seat. I settled into a chair next to her and we giggled like schoolgirls while Skip navigated the schooner out of the harbor and headed for the open sea.

"It's so peaceful out here," my mother said.

I nodded and gazed at the quiet ripples that caressed the ocean's surface. "The calm before the storm," I murmured.

I had no idea how prophetic my words would be.

Once we reached our destination, Skip cut the engines and my father dropped the microphone into the water. When he adjusted the volume, I heard a faint but familiar clicking sound.

"Hear that?" I said to my mother. "It's a killer whale."

Her face lit up radiantly. "I hear it."

We listened in awe to the soulful wailing and agitated clicking. They overlapped in a beautiful, haunting medley.

I squinted at my father. "A pod?"

"A large one too," he said with a nod.

An unexpected bitter breeze gusted across the ocean and my mother and I huddled close together with a wool blanket thrown over our shoulders. After a few minutes, my father joined us and we searched for signs of the pod, but the surface remained undisturbed.

Then the sound equipment went quiet.

Twenty minutes passed by.

I sighed with frustration. "I don't see anything."

All of a sudden, a moaning wail pierced the air.

"It's awfully loud," my mother said.

I smiled. "That means they're getting—look!"

I jumped up, pulled her toward the rail and pointed to a pod that was surfacing about thirty feet away. There must have been at least eight killer whales. The magnificent mammals undulated in the water and headed closer to the *Finland Fancy*.

I glanced at my mother. She was just as awestruck as I'd been on the field trip.

Without warning, one of the whales leapt into the air and a huge wave crashed into the side of the boat. My mother was knocked off balance and sent flying into a deck chair.

My father rushed to her side. "Dani! Are you okay?"

"I'm fine, Jack," she said ruefully. "I think I'll sit down." She stifled a yawn and settled back into her chair.

As I watched the whales approach, the sight of their powerful bodies gliding through the water hypnotized me. They were very curious about us and swam in lazy circles alongside the boat. Sometimes they seemed almost close enough to touch.

"Sarah, don't lean over so far," my father warned.

I ignored him, gripped the rail and stood on my toes. Then I recklessly leaned over and stretched one hand down toward the water. When a young killer whale suddenly surfaced next to the boat, I snatched my hand back and my father laughed.

"She's looking at you," he said, elbowing me.

The whale eyed me, then dove underwater.

"She's a calf," my father explained. "A baby. We've been tracking her the past few weeks. She isn't shy, that one. We've even seen her close to one of the villages."

His comment reminded me of something.

I turned around. "Mom, did you know that Nootka Indians have a legend about killer whales?"

My mother shook her head.

"They believe that killer whales would knock over boats," I said. "And bring the drowned people down to their village under the sea. Then the men would turn into whales and live in the *Village of the Whales*. Neat, huh?"

"That *is* neat."

"Long as they don't take us there," my father teased.

"It doesn't sound that bad," my mother said, shifting in her chair. "Just imagine…swimming under the sea without any worries."

I snorted. "Yeah. No worries until the sharks come."

"Actually a killer whale can scare off a shark," my father said.

I looked at him, surprised. "How?"

"Whales will ram into a shark if they feel threatened," he said, butting me with his head.

That sent us all into hysterics.

For the rest of the afternoon, he gnashed his teeth at us and pretended to ram us whenever there was a long silence. From deep in his throat, he made scary noises that grew louder and faster whenever he approached me.

"Da...dum. Da...dum. Da-dum, da-dum, da-dum!"

It was a good thing I hadn't seen the movie *Jaws* back then or I would have been petrified of the ocean.

That night, after we left the harbor, we bought burgers and fries at *Myrtle's* and took them home to eat. While my father and I wolfed ours down, my mother picked at hers.

"Aren't you hungry?" my father asked.

My mother shook her head. "I'm tired, Jack. I think I'll go to bed early."

I watched her, thinking her behavior seemed odd. My mother was a night owl, often painting until the wee hours of the morning. She rarely went to bed before midnight.

"Good night, Mom," I said.

Halfway up the stairs, she lurched to a stop.

My father pursed his lips. "Dani, are you okay?"

She turned slightly, her face an insipid gray. Her mouth moved, but I didn't hear a sound—except the clatter of my fork as it hit my plate.

"Dani?" My father's voice trembled with fear.

I swear that from that moment on everything moved in slow motion. My father pushed himself away from the table, just as my mother tumbled down the stairs and landed with a thud on the rug below.

"Oh God," he moaned, calling her name repeatedly.

He reached her side, knelt by her body and felt for a pulse. In a flash, he scooped her into his arms and strode to the door.

"Sarah!" he yelled over his shoulder. "Get in the car!"

I followed him outside and stood motionless while he draped my mother across the back seat. When he slammed the door, I climbed in front, terrified by his intense expression. He jumped in beside me, revved the engine and the car squealed out of the driveway.

"Daddy, what's wrong with her?" I asked tearfully.

His face went rigid and the muscle in his jaw clenched. "I'm not sure, Honey-Bunny. We'll take her to the hospital where the doctor can examine her." His eyes darted behind him. "Dani, can you hear me?"

There was no response.

I hugged the headrest and gazed at the limp body of my mother in the back seat.

Is she breathing?

eight

The drive to Bamfield General Hospital seemed endless. By the time we arrived, my mother was coming around.

"What happened?" she asked groggily. "Where are we?"

My father released a ragged sigh. "At the hospital."

"You fainted, Mom," I said, peering over my seat. "And you fell down the stairs."

My father parked the car outside the emergency doors, lifted my mother in his arms and carried her inside. Hospital attendants settled her into a wheelchair and pushed her down the hall to an examining room.

I followed behind, my stomach churning in knots.

Time dragged by slowly...mercilessly.

My father paced the small waiting area while I counted the orange tiles on the wall. So many questions screamed inside my head. What was wrong with her? Was she sick?

Is she going to die?

I wanted to ask, but I was too afraid the answer would be yes.

The clicking of hard soles interrupted my morbid thoughts.

I turned and saw a tall, mustached doctor heading straight for us.

"Mr. Richardson?"

My father nodded, his eyes rimmed with red.

"I'm Dr. Anders," the man said. "Would you mind stepping into—?"

"How's my wife?" my father interrupted. "Is she going to be okay?"

Dr. Anders placed a comforting hand on his arm. "I have a few questions for you. Why don't you follow me? Your daughter will be fine out here for a few minutes."

I watched as the two men disappeared into an office. The door closed gently behind them, but to me it sounded like a thunderous boom. I'm not sure how much time passed before my father walked out of the doctor's office, but I remember the expression on his face. It was a mixture of fear and anger.

"Is…is Mom going to be all right?" I asked as he slumped in the chair beside me.

"Dr. Anders is running some tests, Sarah. He isn't quite sure what happened. I think Mom's just tired—worn out. She's been working pretty hard." He rubbed his eyes and heaved a long sigh.

"Don't worry, Dad," I said, placing my hand in his. "She'll be fine."

He blue eyes studied me. "Has Mom been sick lately? Did she say anything to you?"

I shook my head and picked at a stain on my shirt. "No, not sick really. But she has been sleeping a lot during the day. She told me not to tell you."

"I'm sure it's nothing, Sarah."

He was silent for the next hour. The only time he moved was to glance at the clock or to ask a passing nurse for an update on my mother's health.

When Dr. Anders returned, his expression was grave. "Your wife is awake and responsive. I've asked her some questions so we can determine what's going on. Whatever it is, I'm sure it's nothing serious. Perhaps it's stress-induced." He smiled at me. "What does your mother do?"

"She's an artist," I answered timidly. "A painter."

The doctor scratched his chin. "Maybe she's had a reaction to the paint." He turned to my father. "Is her studio well ventilated?"

"She always has a fan going and her window open," my father replied. "But I can't see the paint being a problem. She's been painting for years."

"Well, let's wait and see, shall we? We should have the test results back by tomorrow. Why don't you take your daughter home and come back in the morning."

"Can I see my wife first?"

"I don't see why not. I'll be back in a moment to get you." Dr. Anders started down the hall, paused and turned back. "Of course, children aren't allowed to visit." He must have read my disappointment because he winked at me and said, "But I'm sure we can find a way to sneak you in—if you promise not to tell anyone."

"I promise," I said quickly, crossing my heart.

He returned a few minutes later and escorted us to my mother's room. The first bed was empty and the other had a white curtain draped around it. Rounding the corner, I saw my mother propped up in bed, her hair freshly brushed. A long tube ran from her hand to a bag hung on a metal pole. A clear liquid dripped from the bag into the tube.

She smiled when she saw us. "My two favorite people."

I reached out to her. "Are you okay, Mom?"

"I'm fine. Silly me, I just tripped down those stairs. But nothing's broken, thank God."

I extracted myself from her grip and watched her fight the urge to sleep. She yawned, closed her eyes, then opened them again.

"We'll be back tomorrow, Dani," my father promised as he leaned down and kissed her on the lips.

"I'll be fine," she whispered.

He nodded miserably. "See you tomorrow."

We walked out of the room and Dr. Anders motioned my father aside. They exchanged a few quiet words. Then my father motioned to me and we left the hospital and my mother behind.

The drive home was silent. We pulled up to our house, climbed out of the car, and went inside. The house was empty without my mother in it.

After my father tucked me into bed, he sat beside me and stared out the window. We both jumped when we heard an eagle's distressed cry. The sound pierced my heart and perhaps his too because he rose quickly and moved toward the door.

"Love you, Sarah. We'll go see Mom tomorrow."

"Goodnight, Dad," I said in a small, scared voice.

The door closed behind him and I was left with my troubled thoughts. *What if my mother has cancer? What if she had a heart attack? What if...*

"Mom'll be fine," I whispered. "She's just tired."

Far away, the eagle cried out again, longing...searching.

I heard its mate answer before I drifted off to sleep.

My mother remained in the hospital for almost a week. My father wasn't happy that Dr. Anders hadn't found the cause of her fainting spell, but I was simply relieved. The doctor took various blood tests, but the results came back inconclusive.

Soon my mother was feeling energetic and there was color in her face once more. She was released from the hospital, given some multi-vitamins and ordered to take it easy for the following week.

"It's great to be home," she said as my father plumped the pillow behind her head.

Propped up in bed, she proceeded to read two novels during the next four days, after promising my father that she would relax. By the fifth day, I noticed she was getting restless. When I returned from school, I wasn't too surprised to find her in her studio, working on a painting.

"Dad won't be too happy," I scolded.

She laughed. "You think I'm going to stay in bed all day? I have no more books to read anyway." She blew me a kiss, her hands covered with burnt sienna and cerulean blue.

I couldn't help but smile. It was great to see her looking so happy...and healthy.

"I'm fine," she promised.

What was I to do? She was the adult.

"Did you get the mail?" she asked suddenly.

"Sorry, I forgot."

I scurried downstairs and went outside to the mailbox. When I looked inside, I saw one lonely letter. It was from Amber-Lynn.

"Darn it!"

Her last letter was still sitting on my desk, unanswered.

Glancing at the new letter, I felt a sense of dread...and guilt. Amber-Lynn missed me. She had already written another letter.

What kind of friend am I?

In my room, I re-read her first letter and promised myself that I would send a long reply. I'd tell her everything. After all, best friends didn't keep secrets from one another. Next, I tore open the new envelope and unfolded a single sheet of paper. Amber-Lynn had picked out some pretty notepaper and had sprayed it with her favorite perfume. She also had enclosed a four-leaf clover that had been dried, pressed and laminated.

I sniffed at the paper, smiling to myself. Then I read the letter.

Dear Sarah,

I've been waiting for weeks for you to write back to me but I guess you're just too busy. I guess you must like it there. I know you've found yourself another friend. Your letters seem to be all about you and Goldie. Well I've got a new friend too. Her name is Pam. She moved in down the road from your old house. So I guess we both have new friends.

Sinceerly,

Amber-Lynn.

Your ex-best friend.

I crumpled the letter in my fist and swiped at the tears that pooled in my eyes. Amber-Lynn had been my best friend for years. And now she had deserted me. How *could* she?

My mother found me lying across my bed, sobbing my heart out. "Sarah, what's wrong?"

Her words made me cry even harder.

"Tell me what's wrong, honey," she begged.

I lifted my head and looked at her. She couldn't possibly understand the pain I was suffering. No one could.

"Please, Sarah," she said, her voice soft and caring.

In huge gulping breaths, I told her about Amber-Lynn's letter.

"That *is* sad," she said, stroking my hair. "I think Amber-Lynn really misses your friendship, honey. That's why she's upset you haven't answered her letter."

"Well, she's got a new friend now," I wailed. "What about me? I thought I was her best friend."

My mother raised her brow. "Who is *your* best friend, Sarah?"

"Well…uh, Amber-Lynn *was*."

"What about Goldie?"

"Goldie's my best friend *here*."

She patted my hand. "So you have a best friend in the States and a best friend here?"

I nodded.

"Then Amber-Lynn can have a best friend there and still have you for a best friend. Right?"

"I guess so. But she said I'm her *ex*-best friend."

"Maybe you need to write her a letter. Maybe you need to tell her that you have lots of room for her as your best friend."

When she went downstairs, I thought about what she had said. I didn't want to lose Amber-Lynn's friendship, so I ran over to my desk and pulled out a piece of colorful paper.

My letter to Amber-Lynn was short and to the point.

Dear Amber-Lynn,

You are still one of my very best friends.

I'm glad you found another friend to hang around with. I really miss you but you're so far away. I'll write you a long letter and tell you all about this place if you're still talking to me. Maybe next summer you can come visit me. I would really like that. I will try to write more. I promise!

P.S. My Mom has been sick.

Sincerely,

Your NOT-ex-best friend,

Sarah XOX

I sealed the letter in an envelope and raced downstairs. My parents had a shelf for all out-going mail and I placed my letter with the rest. I was about to head outside to sit on the deck when I heard a loud crash overhead.

"Mom?" I called. "You okay?"

The silence that followed propelled me forward. In a dazed cloud of fear, I rushed upstairs. When I reached my mother's studio, she wasn't there, so I pushed open her bedroom door.

"Mom?"

My heart skidded to a stop.

My mother was lying on the floor in a crumpled heap next to the bed. Her eyes were closed and I couldn't tell if she was breathing. I knelt beside her and checked for a pulse, just like I'd been taught in lifeguard class. It was very faint.

"What do I do?" I cried out, jittery with panic.

The phone was on the nightstand beside me. I gripped it in one hand and punched in my father's number. It rang five times, then his answering machine picked up.

"Hi, you have reached the office of Jack Richardson…"

I held my breath during his message and anxiously waited for the beep. When I heard it, I began to sob. "Dad! Mom's fainted again. She's on the floor. I-I don't know if she's breathing. Are you there? Daddy?"

I hung up, uncertain what to do next. Then I dialed 911.

"What is your emergency?" a friendly female voice said.

"My mom's fainted," I sobbed. "She isn't moving."

"Okay, honey," the woman said. "Keep calm. What is your name and address?"

I gave her my information.

"Okay, don't hang up," she said. "I'll stay with you until help arrives."

Warm tears trickled down my cheek, but I ignored them.

"Mom, wake up," I moaned.

It seemed like hours went by before I heard the wailing of an ambulance coming up the driveway. Later, I learned that it had been less than ten minutes. When I looked outside, I saw the ambulance lurch to an abrupt halt. Behind it was a familiar car.

Running to the top of the stairs, I waited, motionless.

"Sarah?"

My father pushed past the paramedics and raced upstairs. "I got your message," he said hoarsely.

"Dad!" I sobbed.

He picked me up and carried me to my parents' room. His face was deathly pale while he watched two paramedics prepare my mother for transportation.

I stared at her pale face. She was so still, so lifeless.

"Mr. Richardson?" one paramedic said, securing my mother to a board. "You can follow us in your car."

The two paramedics carried her downstairs. Outside, my father and I watched the ambulance doors slam shut with a resounding thud. In a frenzy of flashing lights and a piercing siren, the ambulance sped away.

My father rushed to the car. "Come on, Sarah. Get in."

I don't remember the drive to the hospital, but I do recall the intense fear in his eyes.

Bamfield General was busy that afternoon. People were crowded in the waiting area and we were forced to stand. Half an hour went by before we saw Dr. Anders. He and my father exchanged a few words—none of which I heard—then the doctor scurried off to my mother's room.

"She's coming around," my father told me.

"What's wrong with her?"

He impatiently brushed a hand through his hair. "They don't know yet. Dr. Anders has ordered more tests. Mom will have to go to Victoria for them. As soon as she's stronger."

I didn't want my mother to go anywhere away from me.

"Why can't they do them here, Dad?"

He swallowed hard. "The tests they want to do are special ones. And they're very expensive."

An hour later, Dr. Anders returned. "Daniella is fully awake and lucid," he said. "Her breathing has stabilized and her pulse is normal. You can visit, but just for a few minutes. We're making arrangements for a helicopter to take her to the Royal Jubilee Hospital in Victoria."

He led us to a small room where my mother was hooked up to a variety of strange, beeping machines.

"Sarah," she whispered, reaching for my hand. Her eyes were shadowed with pain and her grip was weak and shaky.

I leaned forward carefully and lightly kissed her cheek. I was afraid that my actions might hurt her. "Mom?"

She struggled to smile. "I'll be okay."

I didn't believe her. I was petrified that she was going to die, that she would die holding onto my hand. Right there, right then. I tried to be brave, but I couldn't stop the tears.

"I...was...so scared, Mom."

"Don't cry," she pleaded.

I bravely wiped my eyes with my sleeve while my father leaned over and kissed her.

"How are you feeling?" he asked.

She stared at him for a long moment. "My chest hurts a bit."

"We have to keep this visit short," Dr. Anders interrupted. He checked one of the monitors, frowned and adjusted one of the liquids flowing into my mother's hand. "We need to get her ready for transport right away."

I followed my father back to the waiting room. It was oddly silent. The only thing that broke the silence was an occasional sniffle from my father or me.

Ten minutes passed.

Then fifteen.

Still no Dr. Anders.

"Sarah?" a voice called.

I twisted in my chair.

Goldie and her grandmother stood in the doorway.

"We were in town, at the shop," Nana explained. "One of the paramedics came in to buy a basket for his wife. He told us that Daniella had been admitted."

"How's your Mom doing?" Goldie asked me.

"She's going to another hospital for some tests."

Nana reached over and murmured in my ear. *"Hai Nai Yu…"*

Dr. Anders interrupted us. "Mr. Richardson, I'm sorry it took so long. Your wife has just left. She should reach Royal Jubilee in about twenty minutes. She'll be seeing Dr. Terry Michaels."

The doctor and my father exchanged quiet words, then we left the hospital and headed for the car. I walked with Goldie while my father hung back to talk to Nana privately.

I quickly found out why.

"I'm going to Victoria, to see your mother," he told me. "I'll have to stay there for maybe a week. We'll see how things go. Goldie's grandmother has offered to have you stay with them."

"Why can't I come too?" I demanded tearfully.

"I don't know how long I'll be gone, Sarah. And you've got school on Monday. But I'll be back as soon as I can. Okay?"

I glanced at Nana. "Okay."

Goldie linked her arm through mine. "Can I come and help you pack?"

"Sure," I said, suddenly exhausted.

My father dropped Nana off at her driveway and we drove home. Upstairs, Goldie and I stuffed a backpack with enough clothes for a few days. I tossed my bathing suit into it at the last moment.

"Are you sure that's going to be enough?" Goldie asked.

"Dad said I could always walk home and get more if I want."

Her expression turned serious. "Are you…scared?"

I nodded. With a troubled sigh, I glanced around my room, closed the door and followed my friend downstairs.

My father drove us back to Nana's and kissed me goodbye.

That particular day was one of the worst days of my life. I felt almost abandoned by my parents. If it wasn't for Nana and her native wisdom, I think I would have gone insane.

That first night, I sat in the living room with the Dixon family. They taught me about the Nootka Indian ways. Nana told me stories about people who had been injured and then healed by ancient Indian herbal remedies.

"I wish I had some of those herbs," I murmured.

"I think I have something," she said.

She walked over to a cupboard, opened it and rummaged inside. A few minutes later, I heard her grunt with satisfaction.

"This is what your mother needs, Hai Nai Yu. Put it under her pillow and it'll take away her pain." She placed something in my lap. "Don't open it or the magic will escape."

I examined the gift. It was a small, blue cloth pouch tied with a yellow ribbon. I pressed it to my nose and inhaled deeply. It smelled mysterious and fragrant, like the musky vanilla cologne that my father often wore.

"Thank you, Nana."

"You're very welcome, child. And don't you worry about your mother. The Great Spirit will watch over her."

I missed my parents more than I thought possible and the fear of losing my mother consumed me. As Goldie and I prepared for bed, I said a quiet prayer for my mother. I wasn't sure if it was God or Nana's spirits that were listening, so I prayed to both.

Much later, after Goldie was asleep, I stared up at the window and listened to the comforting murmurs of voices below. I could see nothing outside except for the moon. It was full and clear. Even the craters were visible.

Far off into the woods, I heard a lone owl hooting.

It was a long, lonely night for both of us.

The days passed in a blur of anxiety and phone calls. Each night my father called from Victoria to inform us of my mother's progress. He explained that her new doctor had ordered a variety of tests. He sounded very technical as he struggled to tell me what the tests revealed.

"The ECG shows that Mom's pulmonary artery has an increased pressure. Her heart isn't pumping properly. The doctors ran some other tests too—a CT scan and an MRI."

"What does that mean?" I asked impatiently. "Is she going to be all right?"

My father's voice trembled. "It means…that her lungs and her heart are working overtime, honey. It's a condition called *Primary Pulmonary Hypertension*. That's why she's been so dizzy. That's also the reason she fainted."

My heart felt as though it were in a vise. "But they can fix her…right?"

Cheryl Kaye Tardif

There was silence on the other end of the phone.

"Dad?" I held my breath.

"I'm here, Sarah. The doctors are doing everything they can."

I spoke to him for a few minutes longer and he reassured me that my mother would be coming home soon. I asked when, but he couldn't say for sure. After I hung up, Goldie and Nana questioned me about my mother's health. I told them what my father had said, although I couldn't remember the name of the condition my mother had.

Nana gave me a hug. "Your mother is as strong as a Nootka warrior. The spirits will watch over her."

My mother remained in the hospital for over two weeks. Every few days my father drove home. I was so happy to see him, but I fiercely longed for my mother.

One Saturday afternoon while I was walking on the shore with Goldie, I heard my mother's soft voice calling out to me. My head jerked toward the grass and there she stood.

"Mom!" I shouted.

I raced toward her and she caught me around my waist, swinging me high into the air. She laughed, her face slightly pale but her eyes glittering with happiness. She looked beautiful in the sunlight.

"Oh my," she said. "You're getting heavy."

My father joined us at the water's edge. "Don't overdo it."

"I'm fine, Jack. Really, I am." She turned to me. "I missed you so much, Sarah."

She squeezed me and I wondered for a moment if she was ever going to let me breathe. When she did let go, I felt like a whale surfacing for air.

"Hi, Mrs. Richardson," Goldie called out.

"Tell Nana and your parents I said thank you," my mother told her. "I'll drop by for a visit in a couple of days."

With a wave, Goldie headed down the beach. "Sure, Mrs. Richardson. I'm glad you're home."

My mother smiled. "So am I."

"Me too," my father agreed.

My parents gazed at each other, their hands entwined.

"Me three," I whispered.

That evening while my parents were watching TV, I crept into their room with the magic pouch that Nana had given me. I slipped it inside the zippered section of my mother's pillow. Then I gently shut the door and went into my room.

Before climbing into bed, I knelt by my bedside. I prayed that the magic

WHALE SONG

pouch would work—that my mother would be healed.

Unfortunately, neither God nor the Great Spirit was listening.

nine

At first, the pouch seemed to be working its magic. My mother complained that the cold dampness made her body ache, but other than that her 'condition', as they referred to it, appeared to be under control. Most of the time my parents called it *PPH*. Whenever I heard that phrase, my ears would perk up.

A week before Christmas, my father left early in the morning and returned mid-afternoon with a surprise. My grandparents. Nonna Sofia and Nonno Rocco lived in Vancouver, but for the past five months they had been visiting family in Italy.

"Mom, Dad!" my mother exclaimed. "I thought you were still in Italy. What are you doing here?"

Nonno Rocco winked at me. "Visiting Sarah, of course."

My grandfather was a burly man with a wide, infectious grin and snow-white hair. He was always full of jokes and stories. Nonna Sofia somehow put up with him, sometimes clucking at him in reprimand. She was a typical Italian grandmother. She wore her gray-streaked black hair twisted into a bun. I loved it when she visited us because she always cooked her secret family recipes and made cookies and delicious sweets.

My grandmother handed a tin to my mother. "You're too skinny, Daniella. Good thing I'm here. Now...tell me more about this Pulmonary Hyper...thing."

My mother's smile drooped.

"Come," my grandmother said, leading her upstairs.

My father patted my head. "You'll have to give them your room for ten days." He looked worried, as though he thought I would argue.

I smiled. "I'll survive sleeping in the living room."

An hour passed before I saw my grandmother again. And when I did, she looked miserable. Her shoulders slumped and her wrinkled eyes drifted toward me, then darted away.

"Sarah?" she called. "Come see what I have."

WHALE SONG

She had brought me some drawing and art books illustrated by an Italian artist. I politely thanked her and took the books to my room. I enjoyed drawing, but compared to my mother, my figures were one-dimensional sticks with goofy faces. I never dreamt that I'd become an artist like my mother.

My parents invited the Dixons to spend Christmas Eve with us and it was one of the most magical nights of my childhood. They arrived in the afternoon, carrying gifts and freshly baked sweets. While Goldie, Shonda and I played board games, the women puttered around in the kitchen and Mr. Dixon, Nonno Rocco and my father sat outside on the deck and discussed river fishing and deer hunting.

Later, we exchanged Christmas gifts.

I gave Goldie a scented, fabric-covered photo album.

"I can put Robert's pictures in it," she said with a smile.

I was pleased when my parents gave the Dixons a sculpture my mother had ordered from the gallery in San Francisco. Nonna Sofia gave them four jars of her famous homemade spaghetti sauce and a bottle of Italian wine. She received a beautiful basket, a jade pendant and some special tea in return.

"Jack," my mother said. "Can you get Nana's gift?"

My father disappeared for a moment and returned with something that brought tears to Nana's eyes. The painting of the gray wolf and the Indian girl.

Nana squeezed my mother's hand. "Thank you, Daniella. I'll treasure this always."

Mrs. Dixon brought out some beautifully wrapped gifts and passed them to my parents.

"This is terrific," my father said, admiring a new tackle box filled with flashy lures.

"Now maybe you'll catch bigger fish," my mother teased.

She opened her gift and pulled out a pair of silver eagle earrings and a large hand-woven basket. Painted on it was a bald eagle soaring above a spruce tree.

"I love these," she said, her face beaming.

Goldie pressed a small box into my hands. Without waiting for an invitation, I tore it open. Inside was a beautiful, hand-carved silver bracelet.

I didn't know what to say.

"It was carved 'specially for you by my brother Andy," Nana said. "See, *Hai Nai Yu*? This is a mama killer whale and her baby. Because we know how much you love them."

"Nana got it engraved too," Goldie said, her eyes sparkling.

I flipped it over.

The writing on the inside was etched in a beautiful scroll.

To Hai Nai Yu—The Wise One of the One Who Knows.

I heard a sharp *crack* and swiveled my head just in time to see an icicle snap off the roof outside and stab the snow below.

A shiver raced up my spine.

My grandparents returned home to Vancouver in January and the chilly winter months passed by swiftly. By March, my mother appeared to have made a complete recovery. She even went back to painting, although my father cautioned her constantly to take it easy. I'm not sure she knew what that meant. She seemed almost driven by an unidentifiable force. She finished two paintings in record time and started on a third.

One Friday morning, my father joined us for breakfast instead of hurrying off to work like he usually did.

"Want to go out on the schooner tomorrow?" he asked me.

"That's a great idea," my mother said. "I'll pack us a picnic lunch."

My father frowned. "Dani, perhaps you should stay—"

"I feel great, Jack. Quit being such a worry-wart."

Early the next morning, we packed a large basket and drove to the harbor. When we reached the dock where the *Finland Fancy* was moored, I noticed another schooner in her place.

"Where's your boat, Dad?" I asked, confused. "And what's *that* one doing in your spot?"

My father chuckled. "That's her, Sarah."

I eyed him as if he'd lost his mind. "What?"

"She's been refinished, inside and out," he explained. "Looks great, huh?"

Stunned, I examined the *Finland Fancy*. She had been given a fresh coat of paint to see her through the winter months and looked sparkling clean. Her deck had been stained in a cherrywood finish and the hull was painted a pale blue with a royal blue trim.

"Wow," I said, awestruck. "I didn't even recognize her."

"Yeah, me too when I first saw her," he said.

Skip greeted us with a friendly salute, his white hair curling under his captain's hat. He patted me on the head, went to his cabin and prepared to leave the harbor.

"Get Mom a glass of water," my father told me as he untied the moor lines and pushed off from the dock.

I headed below deck to the galley and poured ice water into two glasses—one for my mother and one for me. I took them up top where my father was fussing over my mother.

"Go below if the sun gets too hot," he warned her.

Rolling her eyes, she settled into her chair and slipped on some sunglasses.

WHALE SONG

"Yes, dear."

I released a pent-up sigh. It was wonderful to see her healthy again. Everything seemed normal and I tried to put my fears to rest.

Bundled warmly in blankets on the deck, we listened to the songs of the sea. With the echolocation equipment, we heard numerous fish, a couple of seal lions and at last the familiar sound of the killer whale. My father scribbled constantly in his notebook—seemingly in another world—while my mother and I stared up at the clouds and tried to distinguish shapes and creatures.

"That one looks like a fairy," she said, pointing at a fluffy, cotton candy cloud.

"Or an angel," I added.

We gazed at the sky and watched the fairy angel dissipate until it stretched into an abstract design. It made me think of something I'd been meaning to ask her for a long time.

"Mom, do you believe in Heaven?"

There was an imperceptible tremble in my mother's hand as she carefully plucked off her sunglasses and folded them in her lap. Then she released a long breath and her eyes skimmed across the water.

"I think it must be a wonderful place with no pain or sorrow, a place to be free. Kind of like a big ocean where you can swim around in warm water without fear." Her eyes rested on me. "Why do you ask, Sarah?"

I shrugged. "I just wondered. Nana says that sometimes people can come back as an animal—after they die, I mean. At least that's what the Nootka believe."

"What would you come back as?" my father asked me. "An eagle?"

"No way. I'm too afraid of heights."

My parents snickered loudly.

"I know what I'd come back as," my mother said.

"What?" I asked.

She reached over, picked up the headphones and slipped them over her head. She grinned and passed them to me. At first, there was only silence. Then I heard the soft keening of a whale.

"A whale," I guessed.

She grinned. "Then Dad could study *me*."

Her eyes met my father's and they gazed intently at each other for a long time. I studied them apprehensively, engraving that memory on my mind. Suddenly, I sensed a change in the air around me. It was as if we were in a vacuum. For a second, the breath was sucked right out of me. A shiver ran up my spine.

"And if I was a whale," my mother continued. "You and your father could come out here and visit me every day. But you'd have to learn how to speak *orca*, so we could communicate."

She made short clicking sounds and cried like a whale.

I shrugged off my dark mood and laughed at her giddy behavior. But I felt a lump in my throat when I replayed the conversation in my mind.

"Look!" my father shouted.

My mother and I turned our heads in unison and saw four whales surfacing near the schooner. The pod frolicked in the water and we shrieked when the largest whale lifted right out of the water and slammed sideways on the surface.

Then I spotted something in the distance.

A single killer whale swam about thirty yards behind the pod. It was a calf and it was trying to catch up to the four adult whales.

My father's brow pinched in bewilderment. "That's the same calf we saw last time. But that's not her pod. They have different markings."

Saddened, I gazed at the calf. "Where's her family then?"

He rubbed his face. "She's somehow gotten separated from them. She's still rather young to be on her own though." He flipped through his notebook and jotted something down.

"Will this pod take her in?" my mother asked.

He sighed. "I don't know. I've heard it happen occasionally, but it's not common for a pod to adopt another whale."

At that moment, Skip interrupted us. "I think we should head in, Professor. The winds are changing and we could be in for a storm."

My eyes drifted toward the lonely calf. She followed the other whales, always remaining a safe distance behind them. It was as if she were desperately trying to seek approval from the other pod.

I knew how it felt to be different, to be an outcast.

Two days later, my mother relapsed and was back in Bamfield General. This time she stayed in the hospital for four days and Dr. Anders released her with strict warnings that she was to spend the next two days in bed. He said she needed to rest more during the day and he gave her some medication to take daily.

School had made special accommodations for me during the past month and when I finally returned to class, I was greeted by a warm round of applause from my classmates and Mrs. Higginson.

Everyone seemed to be happy that I was back.

Except Annie Pierce.

On my way to the girl's washroom, I was ambushed. Annie shoved me inside and barred the exit. Her friends remained out in the hallway, guarding the door.

"Think you're somethin' special, don'tcha?" Annie smirked.

I felt like a kitten cornered in a cage with a voracious lion.

"You're just white trash," she muttered as she paced in front of me. "And not even Canadian trash. Why don'tcha go on back to the United States?"

Trembling, I said, "Leave me a—"

Without warning, her foot shot out and connected with my knee. I felt a searing pain shoot up my leg and the next thing I knew, I was shoved to the floor.

"White bitch! You think you're better than me?"

She stomped on my ribs, my arms and my legs.

"Annie, stop it," I pleaded. "Please...you're hurting me."

Her furious eyes narrowed and for a moment I thought she was going to let me go. But she dragged me into one of the stalls and plunged my head into the toilet.

I couldn't breathe. I choked on bitter toilet water and my nose burned. I thought for sure that I was going to drown. My whole life of eleven years flashed before me. *Mom...Dad...*

I began to fight back. I scratched at her arms and stabbed my nails into her skin. When she let out a piercing shriek and released me, I stared at her, terrified of what she'd do next.

"Annie..."

She crouched down by my face. "You're nothing."

My head smacked hard against the toilet bowl and blackness swirled around me. As I tried to stand up, a wave of dizziness overwhelmed me and I fell to the floor. Voices faded in and out, invading the thick fog of my mind. Blurry faces stared down at me, concerned and caring. Then someone lifted me up.

And I surrendered to the painful but welcoming darkness.

ten

"Sssarah…"

I was a butterfly, wrapped in a warm cocoon. I snuggled in deeper, safe and loved. No worries, no fears…

"Sarah, wake up."

I reluctantly opened my eyes and blinked a few times.

The cocoon was gone.

My eyes drifted over my surroundings, recognizing the bay window, my swimming ribbons, my room. I was at home, safe in my own bed. My throat was raw, my head throbbed and every inch of my body screamed with pain. I tried to move, to sit up, but the pain was unbearable.

My father stood over me, a worried expression on his face.

"Daddy?" I whimpered.

"It's okay, Sarah," he said, pulling a chair to the bed. "Don't try to sit up, just relax. You're safe now."

Memories of Annie's savage beating engulfed me and I recalled her pushing my face into the toilet. I had thought my life was over. What had I ever done to deserve such treatment?

I squeezed my eyes shut for a moment. When I opened them again, my father was watching me. His eyes were red and puffy.

"I hurt all over," I murmured.

The door opened and my mother entered, carrying a tray. As soon as she saw that I was awake, she rushed to my side, set the tray down and kissed my cheek. I felt a hot tear land on my chin.

"How are you feeling?" she asked.

Like I've been run over by a logging truck.

But I couldn't tell her that. "I'm…a little sore."

"Nana brought you some of her special herbal tea. She said it'll make you feel much better."

WHALE SONG

Although the tea was sweetened with honey, it tasted somewhat peculiar. But if Nana said it would make me feel better, that was all that mattered.

My mother sat down at the foot of my bed. "Sarah, what happened with Annie today? Why would she do this to you?"

I hesitated.

"Tell us," my father said. "We need to know everything."

So I told them about Annie's bullying. Afterward, they sputtered and fumed, and my father paced the floor. He looked like he was ready to hit something.

"Dr. Anders came to the house to check you over," he said after he had calmed down. "You have a few bruised ribs, a cut on your forehead and some bruises. Other than that...you're fine."

"You call that fine?" my mother asked, outraged. "Look at her, Jack. Annie almost killed her." Her voice broke and she turned away.

My father walked to the window. "Annie's been suspended from school for the next two weeks. You'll be staying home for a few days, Sarah. After that..." He shrugged. "We'll see."

I eyed him warily. "What do you mean?"

"Your mother and I've been talking. We think it would be better for you to go to another school on the island. It would mean a longer bus ride, but at least you wouldn't be bullied anymore."

"But Dad," I argued, struggling to untangle myself from the blanket. "I don't want to go to another school."

"What about this Annie girl?" my mother snapped. "Look what she did to you. Dad and I couldn't believe it when the principal called to tell us what had happened."

"We just want you safe," my father added.

I felt a lump in my throat and my eyes watered. "I know. But what about Goldie and my other friends? I'll be okay...really. I don't want to change schools."

His jaw clenched. "We'll talk about this tomorrow. You just rest for now." He motioned to my mother and they left.

Anxious thoughts churned in my head. I'd be heartbroken if my parents made me move to another school. I would miss Goldie terribly. At that moment, I hated Annie more fiercely than I had ever hated anyone. I felt humiliated that she had beaten me up and that I had not fought back. I berated myself for my weakness, and refused to ever let her touch me again. In my childish heart, I condemned her to a miserable fate and I prayed that she would suffer ten times worse than I did.

"I hate you, Annie Pierce."

My parents said that I could remain at Bamfield Elementary as long as Annie stayed out of my way, so four days later I returned to school. Mrs. Higginson hugged me when I entered the classroom, and Goldie who had visited me almost every day, gave me a card signed by the entire class.

"You've had such a rough time, dear," Mrs. Higginson said to me. "If anyone bothers you again, you let me know."

At lunch, I sat with Goldie and four other girls.

"It sure is quiet without *her* here," my friend whispered.

"You can say that again," I agreed.

She grinned. "It sure is quiet without *her* here."

I elbowed her and we laughed.

Without Annie threatening me, school became a safe haven and I settled into a regular routine of classes and homework. I was becoming one of the more popular girls in the school and I loved that everyone had missed me.

On my second day back, I was surprised to find an envelope stuffed in my desk. Inside was a card decorated with a bright yellow happy face. I opened it and smiled, thinking it was from Goldie.

School is boring without your happy smile and laugh.

I read the signature and blushed.

Adam.

My stomach was tied up in knots and I couldn't look at him for the entire day. *Adam likes me.* I felt a warm fluttering in my stomach, but at almost twelve years old I told myself I was being ridiculous.

As we rode the bus home, I showed the card to Goldie.

"Ah ha!" she snorted. "See? He *does* like you."

She giggled about that card all the way home.

"Wanna ride bikes later?" she asked before I climbed off the bus. "I'll show you around town—unless you're still hurting."

"No, I'm okay now. Bike riding sounds good."

When my homework was done, I rode over to her house and followed her down the winding road to town. Every now and then, she would stop, point at a house and tell me who lived there. I was surprised that some of the kids from my class lived quite close to me.

Goldie braked in front of a large modern two-story with red brick pillars at the driveway entrance. "Denise lives here," she said. "Her dad's rich. He owns two companies and her mom's some kinda brain doctor."

We pedaled past the huge house and down an overgrown gravel road. I detoured around rocks and crumbling potholes and pedaled harder to keep up to her.

"There are two houses down here," she hollered over her shoulder. "But only one is…important." She smirked.

The first house we came to was a small bungalow with a beautiful yard full of wildflowers. A sprinkler sat unattended on the lawn while country music drifted from a kitchen window. A tire swing with a well-worn path below it was suspended off a tree branch.

"Whose house is this?" I asked.

A second later, I had my answer.

"Hey, Sarah," a familiar voice called from behind the bushes.

Adam appeared, carrying a shovel in one hand.

I gaped at him.

His face was streaked with fresh soil and his jeans were torn at both knees. Most of the girls at school thought he was cute and I couldn't help but agree with them. He was my first crush—a crush that lasted an eternity.

"Goldie Dixon!" I hissed. "You are *sooo* dead."

Adam walked over to us, but I wouldn't look at him.

Goldie giggled. "I'm taking Sarah on a tour. Wanna come?"

I jabbed her in the side with my elbow. *What is she doing?*

"I can't," Adam said with a shrug. "I'm helping my mom in the garden out back. We're getting it ready for planting."

"Maybe next time," I murmured as I grabbed Goldie's arm and hauled her back to our bikes.

Adam watched us ride away. I knew it even though I refused to look back.

Goldie grinned. "Hey, Sarah? He's still looking at you."

I smacked her arm and raced off ahead, my cheeks burning with embarrassment.

"Wait up!" she shouted. "Let's head back."

My bike skidded to a halt, sending rocks flying across the road. "I thought you said there's another house up ahead."

"We don't need to see that house. It's not important."

Suspicious, I peered down the road and glimpsed a deserted yard that was overgrown with dandelion weeds and untrimmed bushes. The rusted frame of an ancient Ford pickup truck was parked on the driveway, two of its tires deflated. Beyond the truck stood an old rundown farmhouse that sat broken and uncared for in its graceless presence. A metal screen door hung off one rusty hinge. It screeched in rebellion as a gust of wind caught the door and slapped it against the side of the house.

Goldie's dark brown eyes followed my gaze. "Annie lives there. Just her and her dad. He's a drunk."

Shocked, I stared back at the house. There wasn't a single trace of life. "Where's her mom?"

"They don't know. She took off with some guy a couple years ago—a *white* man."

Annie's spitefulness and hatred of me suddenly made sense.

Goldie nudged me. "Let's get out of here. Before she sees us."

As we sped away, I glanced over my shoulder and saw a shadow pass behind a fluttering curtain in a second story window.

I swear I saw a face peering down at me.

The next time I saw Annie, she was sitting in the principal's office. The door was slightly ajar and I could see her pale face. It was filled with fear. She stared at her lap and didn't even notice me standing out in the hall.

A man's loud, angry voice muttered a curse. "Of course she'll behave. She knows better now. I don't trust her home by herself and I haven't got time to sit around with her all day. A man's gotta work, ya know."

A burly, unshaven hulk paced past the open door.

Annie's father.

Mr. Pierce's long black hair drooped over his shoulders. His clothes were faded, torn and dirty. His black eyes flared as they rested on Annie.

The principal said something I couldn't hear.

"She won't touch that white girl again," Mr. Pierce mumbled.

"Annie can return next week," the principal said.

Holding my breath, I gripped the doorframe and took a silent step back as Annie stood up. When I heard footsteps approaching the doorway, I darted around the corner and hid in the shadows of a trophy case. I clamped my eyes shut and prayed that they wouldn't see me.

They walked right past me.

"Get your lazy ass on home," Mr. Pierce growled.

I saw him grab Annie's arm and shove her toward the exit. When his fist reached back and cuffed her across the back of the head, I gasped in shock. I thought of my father, so kind and gentle...my best friend in the whole world. He would never hurt me like that.

I didn't understand how any father could be so cruel. I was conflicted. The bruised, bullied part of me felt that Annie deserved every bit of abuse for all the pain—both physical and emotional—that she had caused me.

Yet deep in my heart, I felt immensely sorry for the girl.

The following week, I ventured out on my bike alone. Somehow, I found myself parked in the bushes beside Annie's house. I inspected the yard. There was no one in sight and I prayed that nobody would find me spying.

"What are you doing?" I reprimanded myself.

WHALE SONG

I reached for my bike with the intention of leaving, but Annie darted from around the side of the house. I saw terror written all over her face. Then her father staggered out of the house, yelling at the top of his lungs.

"Get back here!"

I was paralyzed.

Like a deer trapped in the headlights of an oncoming vehicle, I didn't dare move an inch. I tried to slow my breathing for fear that they would hear my ragged gasps. Shrinking back into the bushes, I was unable to look away.

Mr. Pierce yanked on Annie's arm. "You're nothing, you stupid bitch. Nothing but a worthless piece of crap."

You're nothing.

I instantly flashed to the day she had beaten me up in the girl's washroom. She'd said those exact words to me just before I had blacked out.

I watched in horror as her father wheeled her around and slapped her across the face. Then he shoved her away and disappeared into the house.

There was complete calm. Not even a bird chirped.

I quietly wheeled my bike toward the road, but then I heard something and looked over my shoulder. Annie had collapsed to the ground, small and broken. I watched as she began to sob hysterically. I was horrified by what I'd witnessed and confused by the mixed feelings I had. I hated her...yet I felt so awful for her.

I took an unsteady step forward.

Snap!

Her shoulders stiffened. She stopped crying, her hand swiping angrily at the dampness on her cheeks. Her piercing glare inspected the bushes, drifting slowly toward my hiding place.

I held my breath, waiting...

eleven

Time stood still while I cowered in the bushes outside Annie's house. I was certain that she would discover me. Thankfully, she vanished inside. I was on my bike and down that road so quickly I didn't even have time to look back. I scrunched low over the handlebars and pedaled frantically—scared that she or her father would come after me.

"Please don't let her see me," I whispered.

When I reached my house, I tossed my bike against a hydrangea bush, ran inside and slammed the door. I leaned against it, panting. "Mom," I called. "I'm home."

There was no answer and my heart skipped a beat. Until I found the note that my mother had left. She was at Nana's.

I darted upstairs to my room and threw myself on the bed.

Should I say something to my parents about Annie?

In those days, people didn't get involved in other people's business. I was a terrified child—an innocent bystander who had witnessed unspeakable cruelty. But back then, I knew nothing about child abuse or the laws that protected children.

What if no one believes me?

I convinced myself that Annie and her father would hunt me down and do horrible things to me if I told anyone what I'd seen. I was sure that people would think I'd made it up to get back at her.

So the only person I told was Goldie.

The following week, Annie was back in school. I caught myself staring at her often and worrying about her father. One time, I caught her glaring back at me. I spent that rest of that day looking over my shoulder. And I made sure that I never went into the washroom by myself.

During social studies, I scribbled a note to Goldie and slipped it to her. She unfolded it in her lap, read it and shook her head.

75

WHALE SONG

The note said, '*Should I tell someone what I saw?*'
In the end, I remained silent...and scared.

Before long, June was upon us and I was ecstatic because that year my birthday fell on a Saturday. *Saturday, June 18, 1978.* School rushed by in a blur of activities and exams. I couldn't wait for it to be over and for summer holidays to begin.

One day, Mrs. Higginson made a surprise announcement.

"On the seventeenth we're going on a field trip."

Everyone cheered and she had to tap her yardstick on the blackboard to settle us down. "Sarah's dad has graciously offered us their beach and raft."

I blushed and shifted self-consciously in my seat. Most of the kids thanked me and gave me looks of approval—but one did not.

I felt hot breath on the nape of my neck.

"Sarah is *so* special," Annie hissed in my ear.

On the morning of the field trip, everyone showed up carrying beach bags. Immediately following our morning math class, we hopped on the school bus and drove to my house.

"Where do we get changed?" Denise asked me as we walked inside.

I showed my classmates the downstairs bathroom. "There's one upstairs too."

Annie leaned against the wall by the bathroom door, a cocky smirk on her face. She was wearing a pair of denim shorts and a t-shirt. In one hand she carried an old, stained towel.

"Don't you have a bathing suit?" Adam asked her.

She waved him off. "I don't need one. I can swim in these."

At the beach, Mrs. Higginson went over her long list of *dos and don'ts* while my father made everyone promise not to swim any farther than the raft. Then Denise, Goldie and I plunged into the water. We were halfway to the raft when Adam swam past us.

He turned his head and grinned. "Race ya to the raft, Sarah."

"No thanks," I said, swallowing a gulp of seawater.

He shrugged and swam off ahead.

Goldie snorted. "You could've beat him."

"Maybe."

"No maybes about it," Denise quipped. "You passed Junior Lifeguarding. I've seen your medals."

"I didn't want to race him...but I'll race you two."

I kicked ahead and went from a relaxed breaststroke to a full speed front crawl. Goldie and Denise didn't stand a chance.

Adam smiled at me as I reached the raft. "Maybe next time."

Wiping the water from my eyes, I reached up to grab the metal stepladder. To my surprise, he leaned forward, grasped my hands and hauled me up. Heat rose in my cheeks and I self-consciously adjusted the top of my new bikini.

"Thank you," I murmured, praying that my friends hadn't seen what he'd done.

When Goldie and Denise reached the raft, they climbed up and flopped down beside me. Goldie glanced at Adam. Then she made a face at me. Her brow arched and wiggled devilishly and I heard the rumble of laughter deep in her throat.

I whacked her and hissed under my breath. "Stop it!"

I was fully aware of Adam. He sat a few feet away and glanced at me occasionally, a strange look in his eyes. I noticed his tanned skin and the muscles developing in his adolescent body. I even noticed a tiny, faint birthmark on the inside of his right ankle.

Denise let out a loud groan. "Oh darn it. Here comes trouble."

I turned and my breath caught in my throat.

Annie was swimming toward us. She wasn't a bad swimmer, but her progress was slowed down by the weight of her shorts and t-shirt.

"Shoot," Goldie muttered. "I was hoping she'd stay on the shore. Maybe dig herself a sandcastle or something."

"Come on," I said, thinking of Annie's father. "School's almost out. Let's just be nice to her for today."

My friends turned and gaped at me.

"I can't believe you just said be *nice* to her," Goldie said. "Are you crazy?"

A few minutes later, Annie joined us. She wrung the water from her short black hair and sprawled in the center of the raft. She ignored everyone except Adam. She eyed him smugly, but he looked away and caught my eye.

"Ah-ha," Annie said, her lip curling. "The white girl has a thing for you."

"Oh shut up," Adam snapped, his eyes glittering.

He stood up and looked at me. "Let's head back, Sarah."

I clenched my hands. I wasn't going to let Annie scare me off my own raft. Was I?

"I'm not ready to go yet...sorry."

Adam shrugged and dove into the water.

Denise gave me an apologetic look. "I'm heading back too. It's too crowded out here." She glared in Annie's direction.

With an unfamiliar pang of discomfort, I watched her slip into the water and catch up to Adam. His laughter was carried in the wind as he teasingly dunked her underwater. When she came up sputtering and giggling, my heart lurched and I realized that it was the sharp tug of jealousy that gripped me. I tried to squelch it, but I couldn't help thinking...

That could've been me he's teasing. Idiot!

Goldie and I sat on the raft in complete silence, not knowing what to expect from Annie. Thankfully, she ignored us. After a while, we relaxed and stretched out on the sun-drenched raft. As we listened to the rhythmic motion of the waves, we were lulled into a quiet calm—just three girls sharing a peaceful afternoon.

I think all of us dozed off for a while.

Something jabbed me and I awoke, startled.

Goldie had rolled onto her side—facing me, her back to Annie.

"We should go." Her voice was low, a bare whisper.

"What about Annie?" I asked.

She shrugged. "What about her? She can stay here or come back. I don't care." She paused. "Is she looking at us?"

I cautiously peered over her shoulder and studied the girl who had become my enemy. Annie was lying on her back, her dark arms folded across her chest. Her eyes were closed and her mouth was curved in contentment.

I was astounded. That was the first time I'd seen Annie smile.

Lowering my head, I said, "Nope. She's just lying there."

After a minute, I stole another peek. My eyes were drawn to Annie's lower legs. They were covered with bruises. Her arms were dotted with small round scars—some faded, some raw and blistered.

Appalled, I dropped my head. "What's on her arms?"

Goldie peeked at Annie. "Cigarette burns."

I shuddered.

Unable to resist, I lifted my head again. But this time Annie's eyes were open and staring directly at me. Her relaxed expression had vanished, replaced by a fierce look that left me rattled.

Mrs. Higginson's whistle blew.

"We should go," I said in a loud voice. "It's lunch time."

Annie scrabbled to her feet. Her t-shirt was damp and wrinkled, clinging to her like a second skin. She strode toward me and stopped a foot away.

"Hey, Goldie," she said, flexing her toes and curling them over the edge.

"Yeah?"

"Race ya to Fallen Island."

I was horrified by her tactless comment, but Goldie just shook her head calmly. "No, it's too far."

Annie's eyes narrowed. "Maybe for Robert."

Without thinking, I whirled around and my fist connected with her arm. I heard her gasp in pain as she toppled into the water. Remembering her bruised and burned body, I flinched. I felt guilty and ashamed that I had added to her agony.

She gripped the side of the raft and glared up at me. "How about you, whitey? Or are ya chicken?"

She didn't wait for an answer. Instead, she started swimming in the direction of Fallen Island.

Goldie stood beside me, her mouth hanging open in shock.

"Annie, get back here!" I yelled.

But the girl ignored me.

"Come back!" Goldie hollered.

We screamed at her, begged her, but she kept going.

"I promised my dad I'd never swim past the raft," I told Goldie as I paced the raft. "But…"

Should get my father or jump in after the girl?

Goldie's fingers dug into my arm. "Where is she?"

Annie was gone.

"Annie…"

I saw a hand thrashing about in the waves.

"Goldie, go get my dad."

My friend stared at me as if she hadn't heard a word.

I grabbed her shoulders and shook her. "Get my dad *now!*"

Without waiting for an answer, I dove into the water and started the long swim toward Annie. By the time I reached her, she was closer to Fallen Island than to the raft. I was a few strokes from her when I realized that her shorts and t-shirt were pulling her under. A churning wave billowed and peaked, and suddenly she was sucked underwater.

I dove under, grabbed her and dragged her up for air.

"Take off your shorts!" I shouted.

"Wha—?"

"Just take them off. They're too heavy."

I watched as she choked on mouthfuls of salty water. With some awkward maneuvering, she was able to free herself from the waterlogged clothes and they quickly sank below, out of sight.

Treading water beside me, she said, "Now what do we do?"

"We swim to Fallen Island. It's closer."

She glanced apprehensively at the island.

"We'll make it," I said.

We swam hard, fighting the waves and the current. I pulled ahead of her and urged her to keep moving. Soon there were more than a few strokes that separated us, but I thought if I kept going, she'd follow me. Then I heard her cry out behind me. Without hesitation, I turned back.

I was too late. Annie's head disappeared beneath the waves.

I swam back to her, but she was gone. I dove underwater and searched for her. My hands met only water and the odd piece of seaweed. I came up screaming. "Annie!"

I was terrified that she was drowning beneath me, so I dove again. Once more I surfaced for air empty-handed.

Where is she?

Something brushed against my legs.

"Annie?"

I took a huge breath, filled my lungs and pushed below the surface. I opened my eyes underwater, ignoring the sharp sting of saltwater. Driving my arms downward, I dove deeper.

Pretend you're diving for rings.

The water was shadowed and murky. I couldn't distinguish anything—just dim shapes and flashes of iridescent light.

Then I felt it. A gentle nudge on my back.

I turned my head. *Oh God!*

Water escaped from my lips as I gazed into the face of a killer whale. I was paralyzed. We stared at each other—nose-to-nose—and I sensed a kind of mutual communication, an understanding. Without thinking, I reached out my hand, unafraid of the huge mammal. As soon as I touched its slick skin, I recalled the dream I'd had the night after meeting Goldie—the dream where I had swam with the whales.

The whale turned, its sleek body rubbing across my legs.

Surprised, I released more bubbles of air. Then my chest began to burn. I looked up with wide eyes, realizing something with impending doom.

The surface was far above me. And I was running out of air.

I panicked. My hands flailed and I fought to get to the surface. It was just beyond my reach.

I'm not going to make it.

My heart strained against my chest. *Puh-pum! Puh-pum!*

Desperate for air, I clawed at the water.

My head felt like it was going to explode.

I pulled upward, reaching.

Toward the light…

Clawing…

But the light was too far away.

I'm drowning. Like Annie…and Robert.

twelve

All of a sudden, I felt myself miraculously lifted, propelled by the killer whale below me. I tightened my body, keeping it streamlined as water rushed past me in a blur.

My lungs strained for air.

Faster!

My head pounded, my heart raced.

Then I saw the light and I broke the surface, gulping in a burning lungful of air. Panting and coughing, I eyed the whale as it lolled next to me, its head above the water.

"Thank you," I said hoarsely.

It stared at me before vanishing beneath the surface.

Then I remembered Annie.

A few feet away, I saw her head bobbing in the water. Determined strokes brought me to her side. I turned her over, grasping her across the chest like my lifeguard course had instructed. Then I swam for Fallen Island, towing her limp body beside me.

"Come on, Annie," I pleaded.

I stumbled to shore and dragged her across the sand. My feet were scraped and bloody from sharp rocks and weather-beaten driftwood. I dropped to the ground beside her unconscious body.

"You're gonna owe me big for this," I muttered.

I tipped her head back, cleared her airway and began mouth-to-mouth resuscitation.

There was no response.

"Breathe."

I filled her lungs again.

Nothing.

"You can't die on me, Annie. Who's gonna bully me around?"

Another breath.

This time Annie reacted.

With a violent shudder, she gagged and spewed up water. She made awful choking sounds while I sat behind her, rocking her in my arms and thanking God and the Great Spirit for saving her.

"That's right," I said, my eyes tearing. "Spit it all out."

When she caught her breath, she realized that I had my arms around her. She jerked away and looked at me, confused.

"How'd we get here?"

"I dragged you. You know, you aren't as light as you look."

"You saved me?"

I shrugged. "I did what anyone would have done."

She shook her head. "No, nobody else would've bothered."

Rattled by her comment, I looked away. "My dad'll be here soon."

An unusual calm settled over us.

Until Annie realized that she was in her bra and panties.

"Where are my clothes?"

"You took them off. Remember?"

She folded her arms across her chest and shook her head.

"It was either that," I said dryly. "Or drown."

"I've been awful to you. Why'd you save me?"

The answer was simple. "Because you needed saving."

Above our heads, a tempest was brewing. Menacing clouds blocked the sun and the temperature plunged. A northerly wind kicked up, blowing icy rain and sand in our faces.

We darted under a patch of trees where we shivered, teeth chattering, chilled to the bone. After a while, Annie shifted and rubbed her legs, flinching in agony when she touched a large, purplish bruise. She looked down at her scarred arms.

"S-Sarah?" Her voice trembled. "My dad—"

"Yeah, I know."

Her head darted up. "That was you the other day? Behind the bushes, I mean."

I nodded.

Annie bit her lip. "Thought so. Saw you ridin' away."

There was a long pause.

"You're right, Sarah. I *am* a bully."

I wanted to say something, but I heard a sound half-hidden by the howling wind. An outboard engine.

Dad!

I jumped to my feet, ran toward the beach and waved my arms in the air—oblivious to the harsh gusts that assaulted me.

"Over here!" I yelled, drenched to the bone.

Annie joined me and we hollered together.

The small boat drew nearer and I recognized the one person onboard. My father. And he was more furious than the raging storm overhead.

"We are so in trouble," I moaned.

Bundled up in warm thermal blankets, Annie and I waited, alone in my living room. My parents returned shortly after seeing off Mrs. Higginson and my classmates. With arms crossed, my mother stood near the rain-streaked window while my father paced angrily in front of us.

Neither of them said a word.

I swallowed hard and glanced at Annie. She appeared as nervous as I was, her bare leg jiggling in apprehension.

I cleared my throat. "Dad, I—"

"What the heck were you thinking?" my father roared. "You could've drowned out there. Didn't I tell you *never* to swim past the—?"

"It's not her fault, Mr. Richardson," Annie interrupted. "It's mine."

My mother cringed and looked away.

"The doctor's on his way," my father said with a frustrated sigh. "And your dad too, Annie."

He didn't notice the shiver that racked her small frame.

But I did.

"You promised me, Sarah, that you would never swim past that raft," my father continued, a harsh edge to his voice.

Annie folded her arms protectively against her chest. "I'm sorry, Mr. Richardson, really I am. It's all my fault." Her mouth trembled. "I was stupid."

"Yes, you were. You *both* were."

My father studied her for a moment. He picked up one of her arms and turned it slightly, his brow raised in concern. He pursed his lips and I knew that he suspected what I already knew.

"Did you get all of these bruises today?" he demanded.

Annie snatched her arm back. "I, uh—"

A door slammed.

"Where's my goddam kid?" a man yelled.

Mr. Pierce staggered into our living room. He reeked of sour beer and cigarettes, and his clothes looked like they hadn't been washed in months.

"Where ish-ee?" he slurred. "That little bitch."

My father's mouth thinned. "Mr. Pierce, watch the language. There are kids around."

The man blinked. "What the hell you talkin' about? She's my kid. I'll talk to her how I want."

When Mr. Pierce noticed me sitting next to his daughter, he scowled. "Get away from that white kid, you worthless piece of—"

"*Mr. Pierce!*" my father bellowed.

My mother strode to my side and pulled me off the couch. Her arms surrounded me protectively and I could almost taste her fear.

"C'mon, Annie," Mr. Pierce growled. "We gotta go home."

He lurched forward, steadying himself against a table. His expression was a combination of defiance and something else, something more primal—fear.

"Outside," my father hissed in a deadly tone.

Standing at least three inches taller, yet weighing much less than Mr. Pierce, my father was no coward. He escorted the man to the front door and I swear I saw Annie's father actually cringe.

I followed Annie to the door, afraid of what her father would do once they reached their house.

"Are you going to be all right?" I whispered.

"Yeah," she mumbled. "Oh and, uh…thanks."

On the porch, we anxiously watched as the men exchanged angry words in the pouring rain. Mr. Pierce tried to walk away, but my father grabbed his arm, restraining him. He glanced at Annie, then yelled something in her father's ear.

I couldn't make out the words, but I know that whatever he said, it made Mr. Pierce's face go white as a ghost. Without a word, the man stumbled down the driveway.

As my father joined us on the porch, Annie slid the blanket from her shoulders and motioned for me to take it.

I shook my head. "Keep it. You'll need it out there."

"I'll bring it to school on Monday," she said. "See ya."

She took off, following her father at a safe distance. At the bend, she turned and waved at me. I waved back.

"Let's get inside," my father said. "A storm's coming."

A sharp crack of thunder vibrated through the sky.

"Yeah," I murmured. "A real big storm."

At the urging of my mother, I invited Annie to my birthday party the following day. I was surprised when she actually showed up at the door, a gift in hand. Some of my other friends from school came to my party too. Denise gave me a new watch with a stopwatch and light. Goldie gave me an ABBA eight-track, a pair of earrings and a poster of the Bay City Rollers. And Annie gave me a skirt to tie around my bathing suit.

WHALE SONG

My mother told me I could have two friends sleep over. The ground had dried during the day so Goldie, Annie and I had a sleepover in a tent in my backyard. We stayed up the entire night talking, playing Truth or Dare and listening to my eight-track. At midnight, we told ghost stories and tried to make shadow creatures. It was a great birthday.

When we went back to school the following Monday, I fully expected Annie to return to her constant torment of me. But she greeted me with a smile at the door and walked me to my desk.

If anyone had told me back then that Annie Pierce and I would become friends after I rescued her from certain death, I would have laughed.

But it happened.

Goldie, Annie and I became known as *The Three Warriors*.

That was my father's brilliant idea. My parents had gone to Victoria to see Dr. Michaels and had seen a movie in the theatre—a western called *Three Warriors*, starring Randy Quaid. That's how we got our name. From that moment on, we were inseparable. We went to matinees at the Rec Centre, had countless sleepovers and spent the summer swimming or walking along the shore.

Annie grew in many ways that year. She became a free spirit and everyone was touched by her vivaciousness. Whenever she came over, I couldn't help but remember my mother's words.

Forgiveness sets you free.

It was strange, but it was almost as if by saving Annie's life I had saved her soul. And by forgiving her, both of us had been set free.

But some people didn't deserve to be forgiven.

Annie's father was arrested in mid-July. The following month, he was sent to prison for child abuse.

I suspected that my father had something to do with that.

At first, I thought Annie might blame me for the sudden departure of her father, but instead she happily moved in with her aunt who lived on the edge of town.

"We need a motto," she said one day. "*The Three Warriors* motto."

But none of us could think of one.

That weekend, when we were having a sleepover at Goldie's house, we acted out the story of Sisiutl. Goldie played the monster, Annie played the warrior and I played a fair maiden who needed rescuing. It was then that I remembered what Nana had said the night she first told me Sisiutl's story.

Great warriors never stop trying.

That became our motto.

Throughout the next year, my mother's health fluctuated back and forth between bouts of dizziness and periods of healthy calm. By the following summer, she found it difficult to stand and paint, so she began pulling up a chair to the easel. Bit by bit, her stamina was stolen from her. Before long she slept more than she was awake.

In September of '79, the *Three Warriors* began grade eight. We were placed together in a classroom with an odd-looking—fresh from university—teacher. Mr. Foreman was short, very scrawny with thinning blond hair and his elbows pointed outwards when he walked. We called him *'Ape-Man'* behind his back. He wore brown thick-framed glasses perched on the tip of his long, crooked nose and he always dressed in open-collared shirts like John Travolta in *Saturday Night Fever*—a movie my mother absolutely adored.

Mr. Foreman somehow survived the first two weeks in our classroom. But the poor man became the target of numerous practical jokes. One day, he hastily departed for home after enduring a grueling day of pranks. Strangely enough, he never returned.

Goldie thought that perhaps it was the chair that had been carefully taken apart, then rebuilt without screws or nails that had done him in. Annie and I figured that he'd simply had enough of walking around with thumbtacks stuck in the butt of his jeans.

Regardless, our class was quite content with a substitute teacher who filled in until the principal could find a more permanent replacement. He found Mrs. Makowski a week before Halloween and she turned our miserable, unruly classroom into one of manners and rewards. She was the teacher responsible for molding my hidden artistic talent.

The first week of November, I brought home a special project and showed it to my mother.

"Mrs. Makowski asked me—just me—to design a poster for the school play," I said proudly. "It's in December."

I set to work on the poster that weekend after borrowing some of my mother's art paper and watercolors. I worked in her studio and she gave me tips and suggestions before she went to lie down. When I was finished, even I was amazed. Romeo and Juliet had never looked so beautiful—or so tragic.

I raced downstairs to show my parents. My father was sitting at the dining room table while my mother sat on the couch. Her painfully swollen feet rested on the coffee table.

I showed the poster to my father first. "What do you think?"

"It's terrific, Sarah. You did a great job."

Beaming, I held the poster up. "Do you like it, Mom?"

My mother managed a smile. "I love it. Mrs. Makowski is going to love it too." Without warning, she clutched her chest.

My father rushed to her side. "Daniella?"

"I'm fine, Jack," she reassured him, her lips faintly tinged with blue. "It was just a sharp pain."

Watching them, I felt a growing suspicion that they were keeping secrets from me, that something was wrong with my mother. Whenever I asked them, they'd always say that she was much better.

But she didn't *look* better.

In fact, she looked much worse. She was sleeping more during the day, her ankles and legs were always swollen and she repeatedly lost her balance. Not to mention the fact that my parents were spending more time in Victoria every month.

I rolled up the poster, tied it with a piece of string and tucked it away in my backpack by the back door. When I returned to the living room, my father was sitting beside my mother on the couch, holding her hands while tears ran down her face.

That's when I knew that something was terribly wrong.

"Mom?" I interrupted. "Is your PPH back?"

They exchanged nervous glances and my mother released a troubled sigh. Then my father scooted over and patted the space between them.

"Have a seat, honey," he said.

I stared at him and saw the agonizing torment in his eyes. It terrified me. I sat down and my stomach twisted into tight knots.

"Yes, Sarah," he said. "Mom's PPH is back. She's...very sick."

The soft catch in his voice broke my heart.

"It's serious, isn't it?" I asked my mother.

She turned away, unexpectedly overcome by a fit of coughing. A thin trail of blood escaped from the corner of her mouth, but she didn't notice.

"It's time, Jack," she said.

My father squeezed her hand and wiped the blood from her face with a tissue. "I know."

"Time for what?" I demanded. "What's going on?"

My heart began to pound and my entire body shook.

"Sarah, honey," my mother whispered. "I-I'm not just sick, I'm..." She turned to my father, her eyes pleading with him.

He moved beside me, clasped my hands in his and kissed me lightly on the forehead. "I wish I didn't have to tell you this."

Then he said three words that completely shattered my life.

"Mom is...dying."

thirteen

Those three small words exploded in my head like a nuclear bomb and I felt the world crumble beneath my feet.

"No you're not," I argued. "You're lying—you're both lying!"

My father reached for me. "Sarah, just hear us out."

"No!" I shoved his hands away and leapt to my feet.

"Sarah," my mother said. "We need to talk—"

Ignoring their pleas, I turned away and fled upstairs to the sanctuary of my room. I slammed the door and threw myself down on the bed, sobbing wildly.

"It's not true. She's getting better. They told me that."

I yanked a pillow over my head and cursed my parents under my breath. But their words echoed persistently in my mind until all I heard was, '*Mom is dying*'.

My parents were liars. My mother couldn't possibly be dying. She was much too young. She had years and years ahead of her.

"*Sarah?*"

It was my father.

"Go away!" I shouted, my voice muffled by the pillow.

I heard the door creak.

"*Sarah?*" he whispered. "We aren't lying."

I felt the bed shift under my father's weight. He stayed with me, silent and motionless, even though I refused to acknowledge his presence.

Five minutes ticked by.

Then five more.

I sniffed back my tears, exhausted…numb. I tossed the pillow to the floor and rolled over on my side, noting the redness in my father's eyes. He'd been crying. My father rarely ever cried.

"This is a very difficult time for Mom," he said, his bottom lip quivering. "For all of us. Right now she needs your love and support."

"Is she really dying?" I sobbed.

"Yes, honey…she is."

He reached for my hand. With a hoarse voice filled with raw emotion, he explained that my mother was given a life expectancy of two to three years. And that was two years ago.

"Mom's condition has rapidly declined and the doctors don't know what to do."

My eyes burned. "There has to be something they can do."

"They don't know enough about PPH. And they're only talking now about possible heart or lung transplants. But that's so far off into the future."

"But what about medicine," I sobbed. "Or an operation."

He shook his head. "They can't do anything more for her."

"You mean we just wait for her to…die?"

"We…wait. And we live." His eyes swam with unshed tears.

That evening, we went outside and huddled together on the padded bench of the swing, my mother in the middle. Our hands were intertwined and our emotions billowed like the crashing waves below us.

For a while, we sat there admiring the full moon suspended over the restless ocean. When the sky darkened and the night air grew cool, no one noticed.

We were together. And that was all that mattered.

We didn't talk about my mother's sickness or her imminent death. No one said a word. We held onto her and onto each other, and as a light mist of snow mingled with our tears, we struggled to find a way to say goodbye.

But how could you say goodbye to someone you loved? How could you go on, knowing that you'll never see them, hold them or talk to them…ever again?

That night, the only sounds we heard were the beating of our hearts and the soothing hum of nature—of life all around us.

The next morning, I called Goldie and she agreed to meet me on the beach. After I scrubbed my face, I braided my hair into two long plaits. Then I grabbed a warm sweater, darted outside and ran down the rocky path to the beach, half-tripping over driftwood and seaweed. When I rounded the bend, I saw my friend standing by the small dock. She was skipping stones like my father had taught her.

"So," she said without looking at me. "What's up?"

She always sensed when something was bothering me. She told me once that she could feel it in her *Warrior* blood.

"I, uh—"

My throat constricted and I couldn't get the words out.

"It's your mom, isn't it?" she asked gravely.

I nodded. "H-how did you know?"

She looked at her sneakers, leaned down and tied one of the laces. "I overheard Nana talking to my dad," she said. "She had a vision about bad spirits hovering over your mother."

I didn't know how to respond to her statement. So I told her the only thing I could. The truth.

"My mom's dying." As soon as the words were out of my mouth, I broke down. My chest ached as wracking sobs engulfed me. "My mom's going to die, Goldie."

Her arms flew around me in a death grip. She murmured words of comfort and she cried with me, cried *for* me and shared my pain. Who would've ever guessed that a dark-skinned Indian girl from Canada and a white girl from the States would have such a strong connection?

I thanked God *and* the Great Spirit for bringing her to me.

Goldie stayed by my side the entire week. When her parents announced that they were taking a trip to see some relatives in Alberta, my heart sunk. But Goldie and Nana decided to remain behind.

On the evening of the Dixon's departure, I had a terrifying nightmare. I dreamt that I was running through the woods, lost and alone, my hands covered in blood. I awoke—gasping for air—and sat upright in the dark. Fumbling for the light, I turned on the lamp and stared at my hands. I breathed a ragged sigh of relief. *No blood.*

Restless and unable to sleep, I started downstairs for a glass of milk. But my parents were in the living room. They were arguing. I paused and hid in the shadows.

"I'm running out of time," my mother said. "Decisions have to be made."

A groan. "You know I can't promise you that."

"But this is what *I* want."

"Dani—"

"Promise me, Jack."

In the silence that followed, I tiptoed midway down the spiral staircase and peered over the side. Scented candles flickered on the mantle, lighting the distraught faces of my parents. Sitting down on a cold metal step, I held my breath and watched them.

"We should let the doctors handle things," my father said. "They know what's right. They believe—"

"It doesn't matter what they believe," my mother interrupted. "They're surprised I've made it this long, considering the shape of my heart and lungs. Do you realize how expensive it would be to keep me on a respirator?"

He bolted from his chair. "The expense doesn't matter, Dani!"

"Of course it does," she said, reaching for him. "You and I both know that they might have no other choice but to put me on life support. I could be there for years. And that would take all of our savings…and Sarah's college money too."

My father leaned forward, moaning in despair.

"Jack, look at me," my mother begged. "I can't paint, I can't dance. I can barely walk from here to our bedroom." She doubled over in a fit of coughing.

I gripped the stair rail and quietly rose to my feet. I wanted to escape. I didn't want to hear any more. But my mother's pleading voice drifted up to me.

"You have to promise me, Jack. I—I know that what I'm asking you to do is morally wrong. But sometimes you have to do what's wrong…to make things right."

"I can't do that," my father argued. "I can't do what you're asking me to do. You know that."

I started back upstairs. Unable to resist, I looked back at them. They stood near the window, hugging each other and staring into one another's eyes. Even from the top of the stairs, I felt their love…and their anguish.

"We're only prolonging the inevitable," my mother said with a sob. "I can't bear for you or Sarah to see me lying there—like a vegetable. If the doctors won't take me off life support, then you have to. Promise me…"

I crept up the last two steps and ran back to my room, the glass of milk and my nightmare forgotten. As I drifted into a troubled sleep, I had one last thought.

I hadn't heard my father's answer.

The next morning, I hurried off to school, carrying the Romeo and Juliet poster I had designed for Mrs. Makowski. When I gave it to her, she praised me for my effort. Years later, I thought of that poster and how ironic it was that our school had chosen a play about tragic love, betrayal, suicide and death.

"I really like your poster," Adam told me at lunch.

My fourteenth birthday was half a year away and my hormones raced every time I saw him. In the two and a half years since I first met him, we had become good friends. I still had a massive crush on him, but we never crossed the boundaries of our friendship. I'll admit I was a bit disappointed.

"Mrs. Makowski is making copies to put up all over town," he added. "Me and Bobbie are delivering them after school."

"Gee, thanks," I said.

Annie and Goldie joined us and we shared our lunches while I told them about my mother. No one knew what to say to me, but that was okay. I had my friends. *The Three Warriors*…and Adam.

After school, he called me away from the bus stop and motioned me to follow him behind a spruce tree.

"I, uh…have something for you," he stammered as he stared at the light covering of snow on the ground. "Call it an early Christmas present." He awkwardly pushed a box into my hands.

It was wrapped with birthday paper and I let out a giggle.

His face went red. "Sorry about the wrapping. It's all my mom had."

I opened the box, self-conscious and excited. Inside was a beautiful crystal sculpture of a mother whale and her baby riding the crest of a wave.

I was speechless.

"I thought it would help you remember your mom," he said.

My eyes watered. I stared at him, not knowing what to say.

He looked over his shoulder, then leaned forward. Before I could utter a word, his lips grazed mine in a sweet first kiss. I closed my eyes—savoring the moment—and when I opened them again…he was gone. I stood there, dazed and confused, my fingertips pressed lightly to my mouth.

A million thoughts assaulted me all at once.

Adam kissed me—my first kiss. Should I feel outraged or happy? I'm not even fourteen yet. My father will kill him.

I heard the urgent blast of a horn and picked up my backpack, placing Adam's gift carefully inside. Then I ran to the bus stop.

"What took you so long?" Goldie demanded.

"Forgot something," I lied.

She pushed me up the stairs ahead of her and we huddled in our usual seats.

"What's that?" she asked, eyeing my backpack.

I looked down.

A piece of wrapping paper was stuck in the zipper.

"Just some paper."

I felt guilty that I had lied to my best friend. *Twice.* But I wasn't ready to tell her about Adam's gift. It belonged only to me—like his kiss—and I wanted to keep it that way. For a while anyway.

I peeked at Adam. He was talking to Bobbie at the back of the bus. He must have felt eyes on him because his head jerked up and he stared at me. Then he grinned at me and resumed his conversation with Bobbie.

Flushed, I slunk low in my seat and faced the window, my fingers pressed to my lips, remembering his kiss. Then I smiled and let out a long dreamy sigh.

Luckily, Goldie wasn't in the mood to talk.

The bus rumbled down the road and lurched to a stop in the slushy snow in front of my driveway. With a quick wave to everyone, I jumped off and ran to my house.

My mother was curled up on the couch, fast asleep.

I tiptoed past her and crept upstairs to my room. After I shut my door, I carefully removed the sculpture from my backpack and placed it on the bedside table. Then I scrambled onto the window seat and stared at the whales for a long time.

I thought about Adam. I thought about his kiss. *My* kiss. I turned my head, pursed my lips and pressed them against the icy window. *Adam...*

"Sarah, what on earth are you doing?"

Guiltily, I jerked myself away from the glass and whirled around to face my mother. She was leaning against the frame of my door, a look of amusement on her face. Her gaze rested on the ornament. "What's that?"

"Uh...a friend gave it to me. For Christmas."

Her eyes found mine and she smiled knowingly. "But Christmas is over a month away."

I wanted to tell her about Adam and about the kiss, but I was confused and unsure. I thought she'd be angry with me. Or maybe ashamed. So I decided to tell her later—when the time was right.

I shouldn't have waited.

Two weeks later, my mother was rushed to the hospital after collapsing on our driveway. An ambulance carried her away to Bamfield General where she was immediately transported by helicopter to the Royal Jubilee in Victoria. She had suffered right ventricular failure and both of her lungs had partially collapsed. By the time my father, grandparents and I reached Victoria, she was fading in and out of consciousness.

Dr. Michaels warned us that my mother was stabilized but in critical condition. She took my father aside and whispered something to him. Whatever she said, I knew it wasn't good.

We were allowed to visit my mother, but all I saw were massive machines and endless wires hooked up to every part of her body. An oxygen mask covered her mouth. Her eyes were closed and we heard the soft puffing of the respirator and the unsteady beating of her heart on the monitor.

Puff...puff...

My father stepped toward the bed. He lifted one of my mother's hands and rubbed his thumb along the side of her wrist, barely grazing the intravenous tube that was injected under her skin.

"What did Dr. Michaels say?" I asked fearfully.

"She's worried Mom may become...comatose."

"What's that?"

"A coma is like...a very deep sleep."

I nodded robotically, my emotions shifting into neutral. This had to be a dream. None of this was real. It couldn't be. Maybe if I pinched myself hard enough I'd wake up.

I pinched my arm. Hard. It stung and I stared at the red mark left behind, realizing that I was trapped in my own deep sleep, in a horrific nightmare from which I'd never wake up.

We remained at my mother's bedside for hours, waiting for her to open her eyes. Dr. Michaels and a handful of nurses checked on her constantly, but we barely noticed them.

Nothing existed—except my mother.

We stayed at a motel, leaving early each morning and returning late every night. Dr. Michaels encouraged us to talk to my mother every time we visited, regardless if she was awake or not. I often saw Nonna Sofia hovering over her and whispering in her ear.

On the fourth afternoon, I sat on the other bed and stared out the window, lost in my own little world, while my father and grandparents reminisced about my mother. When I overheard some of their comments, I silently fumed. They were acting as if she were already dead and buried.

"I'm going to grab a coffee and talk to the doctor," my father said, stretching his long, cramped legs. "Do you want anything, Sarah?"

"I'm okay."

"We'll go with you," Nonno Rocco said, motioning Nonna Sofia to follow him.

The second they left, I opened my backpack and took out the package Goldie had mailed me. Adam's gift. Scooting off the bed, I placed it on the table by the window. Sunlight reflected off the sculpture's crystal surface and in the dazzling light, the mother whale glowed as her baby cuddled close to her side.

Suddenly, I sensed a shift of energy in the air—a movement.

Something.

I turned.

My mother's eyes were open. She stared at the sculpture, then her gaze drifted toward me, her lashes fluttering helplessly.

"Mom?" My voice sounded like it was a million miles away.

I moved to her side and saw her hand twitch.

She pointed to the ornament.

I leaned down, inches from her face. "Adam gave it to me."

I'm positive she smiled and a hesitant smile lit my own face.

"When he gave it to me," I whispered. "He…kissed me."

I studied her carefully, memorizing every line and angle of her beautiful face. Her brown eyes drifted shut and her mouth moved. Leaning over her, I thought I heard her say something. I hugged her fiercely, rested my head on her chest and listened to the faint beating of her heart. *Puh-pum, puh-pum…*

I dozed.

WHALE SONG

Puh-pum...puh...

Pummmm—

I was woken abruptly by an alarm shrieking in my head. A flurry of activity surrounded me as the doctor and two nurses flew into the room.

"Take Sarah outside," Dr. Michaels ordered. "Now."

A large-framed nurse peeled me away from my mother and I was escorted to the hallway. I stood outside the door and waited alone, trembling with apprehension. When I heard something crash to the floor, I jumped.

"Sarah!"

My father ran down the hall toward me, my grandparents not far behind. An attendant blocked the doorway to my mother's room. She told my father that he couldn't go inside. I saw the torment and terror in his eyes. Then he crumpled into a chair, helpless and afraid.

"Mom woke up," I said woodenly.

He didn't answer.

Frantic with fear, I strained to hear what was going on inside the room. The alarm had stopped screaming and I heard Dr. Michaels issuing abrupt commands. Twenty minutes later, she walked out of the room. Her expression was bleak.

"Daniella is in a coma."

My grandparents sat stone still. My father too.

The door to my mother's room opened. I saw a nurse leaning down to pick something up off the floor. The woman glanced at me, a sad look on her face. Then she frowned at the floor and my eyes followed.

I sucked in a breath and jumped to my feet. *"No..."*

My beautiful crystal ornament was in pieces—destroyed.

Dr. Michaels touched my shoulder. "I'm sorry, Sarah. We accidentally knocked it off the table in all the confusion."

I rushed toward the door, but my father grabbed me.

"It's broken," I wailed. "You have to fix it."

The nurse carefully collected the shards of glass and wrapped them in a white cloth. Placing it on the table beside me, she crouched by my chair. "All it needs is a little glue, honey, and it'll be right as rain."

I knew the woman was trying to be kind, but all I thought of was how awful my life was.

"Nothing will ever be right," I said with a sob.

Devastated, my father and I returned to our motel room. I crawled into bed and fell asleep while he sat hunched over the desk with a bottle of glue in one hand and the shards from the shattered sculpture in the other. He painstakingly glued every broken piece back together again. Then he set the ornament on the nightstand so that it was the first thing I saw the next morning.

All it needs is a little glue...

Years later, my father told me how he had crept outside the motel room and collapsed—sobbing—against the door.

Nana showed up at the hospital the next day and she wisely took me away from all the machines and chaos. We bundled up warmly, strolled across the street to a park and sat at a picnic table under the trees near a small fountain. Seagulls squawked nearby, fighting greedily over scraps of food someone had left behind.

"Mom's not going to wake up, Nana," I said anxiously.

She nodded. "Yes, *Hai Nai Yu*. The Great Spirit is ready to take her home." She took both my hands in hers. "It is time, little one. Time to let her go so that her spirit can fly free. You have to be willing to release her. Or she'll be trapped between both worlds."

"But, Nana," I moaned. "I don't want her to go."

I lowered my head to the table and tears began to flow. I was lost in a world of pain and suffering, yet all around me was life. I heard children laughing, birds singing and the fountain bubbling.

And I resented them all.

"Have I told you about *Seagull and the Coming of Light*?" Nana asked, her frail hand stroking my hair.

I shook my head against the table.

"The Great Spirit gave the First People small, carved cedar boxes," she began. "One filled with water that rose to the sky and formed clouds. The clouds emptied onto the ground and created streams and rivers. Another box held all the mountains and another held the seeds of every growing thing. The next box held the wind, which blew the seeds and scattered them throughout the Earth. They all opened their boxes. Everyone, that is, except Seagull."

I raised my head slowly. "How come he didn't open his?"

"Seagull wasn't ready to give up his box. He wanted to keep it all to himself. He held his box tightly, refusing to open it. And in his box, he held all the light of the world. And that is why, in the beginning, there was only darkness."

She paused and we watched a lone seagull cautiously waddle toward us. It stopped from time to time and cocked its head to one side, staring at us.

"So what happened, Nana?" I asked, eyeing the bird.

"Well, the First People asked Raven to talk to Seagull. But when Seagull still refused, Raven wished that a thorn would pierce Seagull's foot. And because whatever Raven wished came true, Seagull found a thorn in his foot. Raven offered to help him, to pull out the thorn, but instead of pulling it out Raven pushed the thorn in farther. Then he said, 'If only I had some light to see.' And do you know what Seagull did?"

"He opened his box."

"Yes, *Hai Nai Yu*. He opened his box just a bit and the Stars fell out and lit up the sky. Then Raven pushed the thorn in even farther and told Seagull there still wasn't enough light. And Seagull opened his box some more and the Moon floated up to the sky. One last time Raven pushed in the thorn and Seagull cried out, dropping his box, which opened and released the Sun. And so it came to pass that there *was* light." She paused when the seagull near our table let out a shrill cry and flew away. Then she added, "Seagull learned a valuable lesson that day."

"What?"

"He learned that sometimes holding onto things only brought suffering." Her eyes fixed on mine and I shivered.

I thought about Seagull all day.

When my father and I returned to the motel, I shared Nana's story with him. Afterward, he tucked me in, kissed my forehead and wearily climbed into his bed.

"Goodnight, Sarah," he called from the dark.

I stared up at the ceiling and listened to the unfamiliar sounds around me. I heard rowdy voices outside, followed by thunderous footsteps that clanged up the iron staircase. A car drove past—squealing its tires—and its headlights illuminated our room for a moment.

I held my breath, my pulse quickening.

As I clutched my pillow, darkness engulfed me and I slept. I dreamt of Seagull and Raven. And my mother. I walked with her and held her hand. Even in my dream, I understood that I must find the courage to let go.

Release her or she will be trapped between both worlds...

PART TWO

Trail of the Wolves

fourteen

My mother passed away peacefully on November 29, 1979, less than four weeks from Christmas. But it was the way that she died that permanently altered my life.

Nonno Rocco and Nonna Sofia had gone for a walk outside, leaving my father and me to visit with my mother. When Dr. Michaels arrived, my father asked her to step into the hall.

Overwhelmed by curiosity, I pressed my ear against the door.

"We have to leave her on life support," I heard Dr. Michaels say. "I know that's not what she wanted, but as long as there's brain activity, it's my obligation to keep her alive. I hope you understand that. You can go to the courthouse and file a petition to have her removed—"

"But that could take months," my father argued. "Years."

He grew more insistent and I heard Dr. Michaels ask him to lower his voice. Their indistinct whispers frustrated me. Then I heard them moving closer and I backed away from the door. When they entered the room, my father looked very upset.

"I'm sorry, Mr. Richardson," Dr. Michaels said, checking the monitors. "But I have no other choice." She left the room.

My father heaved a sigh of frustration. The respirator that breathed for my mother imitated him. *Puff...puff.*

"Dad?" I said, shifting in the chair. "I, uh...overheard you talking to Mom the other night."

His brow furrowed in confusion. "What about?"

"I know what she asked you to do."

I saw his face crumble before me, shocked. His head dropped into his hands and a shudder moved up his spine. Slowly, he raised his eyes and studied my mother's immobile body as the machines pumped life into her.

"Sarah," he sighed, shaking his head sluggishly.

WHALE SONG

I remembered my mother's words to him. *Sometimes you have to do what's wrong...to make things right...I can't bear for you or Sarah to see me lying there—like a vegetable.*

I glared at him, angry and betrayed.

Time stood still. Frozen.

Fear held us captive. We were caught in an emotional tug-of-war. My father battled with his conscience while I fought to convince him to set her free.

This is where my world collides—where my memory ends.

I vaguely recall the sound of a door slamming. I must have left the room. The next thing I remember is seeing my father by my mother's bed, holding her hand. In the other, he firmly gripped the unplugged end of the respirator. The monitors were silent, their buttons turned off.

"Sarah!" he shouted in a hoarse voice, his blue eyes piercing me where I stood.

Uttering a cry of horror, I raced from the hospital room and ran down the hallway. I twisted down one corridor and turned down the next until I was lost. I had no idea where I was going. I just needed to escape. *Run, Sarah!*

I collided into a familiar body.

"*Hai Nai Yu*, what's wrong?"

I looked into Nana's eyes, silently pleading for help. Then a merciful darkness encompassed me and I felt myself plunging into its shadowy embrace. *Take me away...*

Sarah!

I heard my mother whispering to me and felt her lips caress my forehead. I smiled. Then I cautiously opened my eyes. There was no sign of her. The room I was in wasn't familiar either. I looked around and realized that I was in the hospital, lying in one of the beds.

That confused me. I wasn't the one who was sick.

Nana sat in a nearby chair.

"*Hai Nai Yu?*"

Her gaze was intense and she frowned when she touched my forehead. "You're too warm."

"Nana, what happened? Why am I here?"

She muttered something under her breath. "Do you not remember, child?"

I shook my head.

"Your mother has gone to the Great Spirit. She's on her way home."

I shook my head in denial and clamped my eyes shut. But the truth hit me with the finality of a door slamming shut.

My mother was dead.

"What happened in her room?" Nana rasped.

I shook my head, confused. "What do you mean?"

"Did your father—?" She broke off as footsteps approached.

The door opened abruptly and my grandparents rushed into the room, their faces fearful and pale.

"Sarah!" Nonna Sofia cried. "Are you okay?"

Nana stood slowly, nodded to my grandparents and slipped from the room. Nonno Rocco moved closer to my bed. His beard was thick and white, and it looked as if he had slept in his clothes.

"What happened?" he asked me.

"I don't know."

I recalled being in my mother's hospital room and then…nothing. Until I woke up.

Nonna Sofia shook her head sadly. "We just want to know why your father did what he did. We know it had to have been an accident, even though the police are questioning him."

"The p-police?" I stammered. "What do you mean? What did he do?"

My grandparents exchanged anxious looks.

I tried to force myself to remember, but everything was so hazy. The only thing I understood with absolute certainty was that my mother was gone. I would never see or talk to her again.

"I want my dad!" I wailed.

Nonno Rocco enveloped me in his arms and I smelled the comforting scent of his cologne.

"Your papa…" he said slowly. "He cannot come here now. He has to…explain what happened."

"I'm sure he'll be here later," Nonna Sofia added.

My grandfather shot her a warning look.

"Well, he will," she said, crossing her arms defiantly.

I slept for the remainder of the afternoon. At some point during the day, my subconscious collected and stored precious tidbits of information. My grandparents and Nana must have been talking while I slept.

"They're calling it a suicide."

"The police…murder."

"Jack might go to prison."

My father had been found beside my mother, holding her lifeless hands in his. He had disobeyed the doctor's orders and had shut down all the monitors and shoved them against the wall. When the alarms rang, a crash cart was pushed into the room and attempts were made to revive my mother. But they were too late to save her.

101

Dr. Michaels had no choice but to call security and have my father quarantined. When the police arrived, they escorted him out of the hospital and questioned him relentlessly for over an hour.

"They even searched him," Nonno Rocco said as I drifted in and out of sleep. "The police wouldn't let anyone into Daniella's room after they pronounced her dead—not even the doctors. They're taking her to the Coroner's Office. My *bella figlia*!"

Through a haze of half-sleep, I heard Nonna Sofia. "Rocco, our beautiful *carina* is gone to the angels. What has Jack done?"

Her keening wail broke my heart.

Merciful sleep rescued me from hearing anything more.

Dr. Michaels came to see me after supper.

"You have hysterical amnesia, Sarah," she said. "It's common after a traumatic event like…this. But luckily it's only partial amnesia."

She was right about that. I remembered everything before she left my mother's room and everything since waking up in the hospital. But I was missing a section of time in between.

Dr. Michaels told my grandparents and Nana that I had to remain in the hospital overnight and that she would locate someone near Bamfield to help me regain my memory.

"Sarah's memory will return," Nana said, nodding. "It'll return on its own when she is good and ready to remember."

The following afternoon, an attendant wheeled me down the hall in a squeaky wheelchair. He pushed me to an awaiting taxi where my grandparents and Nana were exchanging a few words.

"I'm going home now," Nana said, kissing me goodbye.

My grandparents and I took the taxi to a motel.

"We have to go to the police station tomorrow morning," my grandfather said as he tucked me into bed.

I was surprised and a bit scared. "Why?"

"They want to talk to you, ask you a few questions."

"I'm tired," I mumbled, not wanting to think about it.

Snuggling into the crisp sheets, I fell into an exhausted sleep while my grandparents hovered over me, muttering in Italian.

The Victoria Police Department buzzed with activity and everything gleamed with power—especially the gray marble floor. Officers in immaculate uniforms busied themselves with various tasks. Phones rang persistently, fax machines faxed and two young men were escorted past us in handcuffs.

My eyes flitted over them in fear and I wondered if my father was locked up in a jail cell packed with vicious killers—like I'd seen on TV. I followed my grandparents, my shoes tapping noisily across the floor.

At the information desk, Nonno Rocco spoke to a detective.

"We're here to see our son-in-law Jack Richardson," he said. "After we talk to Sgt. Washinski."

"I'll take you to him," the gruff-looking detective said in a thick French accent. "Follow me, please."

He directed us to an interrogation room, motioned us inside and returned to his duties, leaving the door ajar. The small room was harshly lit with glaring fluorescent lights. Four rickety chairs and an old metal table were the only objects in the room that was barely eight by eight feet wide. The carpets were threadbare and stained with numerous suspicious-looking marks. The pallid blue paint on the pitted concrete walls flaked like badly sunburned skin and the air smelled like musty mould and stale cigarettes.

A tall, thin detective with pale blue eyes entered the room. He had a long, bushy brown mustache that curled up at the ends. His uniform was spotless and intimidating, especially to a girl my age.

"My name is Sergeant Washinski," he said with a smile.

He dragged a chair across the floor. Sliding into it, he casually folded his arms over his chest, stretched out his long legs and crossed them at the ankles.

"You must be Sarah," he said in a friendly manner. "Have a seat." He indicated the chair directly across from him.

I glanced at Nonno Rocco and Nonna Sophia. When my grandfather nodded, I sat down.

Sgt. Washinski's eyes sought mine. "Sarah, I know this is difficult, but I need to know exactly what happened in your mother's hospital room, what you saw. Okay?"

"Okay, but—" My voice caught in my throat, as if a noose were slowly tightening around my neck, strangling the air from my lungs.

The detective uncrossed his arms, reached over and turned on a small tape recorder. "Can you please tell me your full name?"

"S-Sarah Maria R-Richardson," I stammered.

He picked up a pen and notebook. "And your mother was in Bamfield General because…?"

"She was sick. She has—*had*—a problem with her heart."

"What happened yesterday?"

I closed my eyes. "Mom was in a coma…"

"Were your grandparents with you, in your mom's hospital room?"

I nodded and opened my eyes.

He smiled. "You're doing just fine, Sarah. But I need you to answer out loud. Okay?" He made a few marks in his book. "Who was in the room with you?"

"Just me and my dad, I think."

"Did your dad do anything—to the machines, I mean?"

My head snapped up. I flicked a panicked look in my grandparents' direction. They looked miserable and Nonna Sofia's eyes were filled with tears.

"I, uh…" I said slowly. "I don't remember."

"Where was your dad standing?"

A sense of dread overwhelmed me and I looked up at the detective. "I don't know."

"What was he doing by your mom's bed?"

"I never said he was by her bed," I said, frustrated.

He pursed his lips. "Where was he then?"

"I don't know," I muttered. "I don't remember."

Nonno Rocco pursed his lips in anger. "Sgt. Washinski—"

"I'm sorry, Mr. Rossetti," the detective said, waving a hand in the air. "But I have a few more questions." He stared at me compassionately. "Sarah, can you tell me what your dad did first? Did he turn off the respirator—the machine that helped your mother breathe? Or did he turn off the heart monitor?"

His questions made me furious.

"I don't know," I snapped, rising to my feet. "I told you. I don't remember anything."

My grandfather was at my side immediately. "We're done," he said through clenched teeth. "Sarah doesn't remember. She has amnesia. Ask her doctor."

Nonna Sofia pulled me protectively to one side of the room and murmured soothing words. I heard an odd ringing in my ears and for a moment, I thought I was going to pass out.

Sgt. Washinski turned off the tape recorder and set down his notebook. "I apologize, Mr. Rossetti," he said. "But Sarah is an eye witness and I had to question her." He walked to the door, paused and glanced over at me. "I'm very sorry about your mom. And I'm sorry I had to ask all those questions. I'll get your dad. You can visit for a few minutes." He disappeared into the hall.

My grandparents and I waited in complete silence. I had a booming headache and I massaged my temple, praying that we'd be able to leave soon.

The door opened and my father entered, thankfully unshackled. He was slightly disoriented, his clothes were wrinkled and his unshaven face was haggard. He looked like he hadn't slept in months.

"I'm so glad to see you," he said as he hugged me.

His grip suffocated me and I squirmed until he reluctantly released me. Then

I flopped into a chair and scowled at him.

"When are you getting out of here? I want to go home."

"Soon, Sarah," he said. "They aren't sure if they're laying any charges, so I just have to wait." He threw my grandfather an uneasy look. "It could take a few more hours."

I wanted to go home with my father, home to the safety of our house on the bay. But I was terrified of going home without my mother.

"Sarah, I have something important to ask you," my father said seriously. "Do you remember anything about what happened in Mom's room?"

I turned away. "No. Not really."

"Are you sure?"

"Jack, we've asked her already," Nonna Sofia said. "The doctor says she has hysterical amnesia. She doesn't remember a thing."

My father sank into a chair. "Well, then they won't ask her to testify." He let out a relieved breath.

"You really think this'll go to court?" my grandfather asked gravely. "And they want to charge you with—"

"Rocco," my father warned, shaking his head. He eyed Nonna Sofia. "I want you to take Sarah home, back to Bamfield. I should be out of here in a couple of hours. They can't hold me much longer without charging me. Can you stay with her until I get back?"

"Of course we'll stay with Sarah," she huffed.

"Thank you. Both of you."

Nonna Sofia stared at my father. In a voice filled with emotion, she said, "Don't you worry, Jack. We'll look after Sarah 'til you come home."

The door opened and a police officer obstructed the doorway.

"I love you, Sarah," my father said as he was led away. "I'll be home tonight, I promise."

Nonna Sofia tried unsuccessfully to console me on the ride home while Nonno Rocco drove slowly along the gravel road, swerving around potholes. None of us felt like talking or eating, and the journey home seemed to take forever.

I pressed my forehead against the cold glass and recalled the first time I had made the trip to Bamfield. My parents and I had been so excited about our new life. I thought of my mother's laugh, her touch, her smell. I remembered seeing the ocean for the first time and being so excited. Now I realized it was only water.

My father's face swirled before me. *What have you done, Dad?*

As I stared out the car window at the passing scenery, I wondered why the two people I loved and needed the most had been taken away from me.

WHALE SONG

I was abandoned. Lost.

fifteen

In Bamfield, a heavy downpour of rain and murky gray clouds spitefully greeted us. The weather seemed appropriate, considering our miserable mood. We drove up the driveway to the house, but it was devoid of life—deserted and silent.

I ran inside and gazed around the living room. The plants were parched and withered, but I ignored them. On a small table was a photograph of my mother—healthy, happy and beautiful.

I stared at her and breathed in deeply.

My mother's spirit was everywhere. I saw her all around me. She was in everything—her painting over the wood stove, her coffee mug on the table and the blue scarf on the chair back. Her perfume still lingered in the air, teasing me.

Upstairs, I unpacked my suitcase and tossed my clothes into a drawer. After a moment's hesitation, I grabbed the phone in the hallway and dialed Goldie's number.

No one answered.

Doesn't Goldie know I need her?

Wandering back to my room, I curled up in the window seat and watched the storm wreak its vengeance. Depressed and lonely, my heart ached.

I grabbed a book from a shelf and attempted to read it, but insidious thoughts kept invading my mind. After a half-hour, I gave up and wandered down the hall. When I reached the bottom of the stairs, someone called my name.

I was shocked.

The entire Dixon family was waiting for me with open arms, their eyes full of concern. Goldie's parents hugged me, and little Shonda gave me a sticky kiss on the cheek. Then Goldie rushed over and wrapped her arms around me, her face streaked with tears.

"I'm sorry about your Mom," she whispered.

Nonna Sofia ushered the Dixons into the dining room and I started to follow them, but Nana pulled me aside.

"Your mama's gone to the Great Spirit," she said. "But we will remember her, *Hai Nai Yu*. We'll have a special ceremony on the beach—to remember her spirit."

They stayed until suppertime, sharing quiet stories and memories of my mother. I knew that if she were watching us she'd be very happy. After all, Goldie's family was part of ours—we were all connected.

When they left, I helped Nonna Sofia make a light supper of chicken and salad. Just as we were about to eat, we heard a car horn. I ran to the kitchen window and saw a taxi drive up on the cement pad. My father got out, looking haggard and worn.

"Dad's home!" I shouted.

The door slammed and my father rounded the corner and swept me into his arms. He hugged me so tightly I thought he would never let me go.

"I missed you so much," he said.

"There's going to be a special service on the beach by the Dixon's house later tonight," Nonna Sofia said softly. "They want to honor our Daniella. Isn't that wonderful?"

My father bowed his head, choking back his emotions. "It's perfect. Daniella would have loved that."

After supper, the adults argued about funeral arrangements for my mother. Nonno Rocco was adamant that my mother should have a proper burial and Nonna Sofia wanted a church service. No one asked me what I wanted. So I watched and listened, wanting only for my mother to return to me—alive.

"We'll have to have a proper Catholic funeral," Nonno Rocco said grimly. "And a burial in a Catholic cemet—"

"Actually, Rocco," my father interrupted. "Daniella didn't want anything formal. She wanted to be cremated and have her ashes thrown into the ocean.

Nonno Rocco's eyes narrowed. "What is this nonsense?"

"Daniella wrote down her wishes. Before she ended up back in the hospital. I'll show you."

My father left the room for a moment, returning a few seconds later with a folded piece of paper. He passed it to my grandparents.

"Rocco," my grandmother said. "It's like Jack says. We have to do what our *carina* wanted."

"Maybe Skip could take us out on the *Finland Fancy*," I said.

My father smiled. "That's a great idea, Sarah. And we'll look for some killer whales—"

My grandmother gasped. "What, you're going to feed Daniella to the whales? What are you thinking, Jack?"

"She loved the whales." He looked at me. "Right, Sarah?"

I stared out the window, watching waves crash upon the beach. "Mom always said she'd come back as a whale."

Finally, everyone was in agreement. My mother's ashes would be spread out over the ocean amidst a pod of whales.

The adults discussed the plans quietly, while I mindlessly watched The Carol Burnett Show on TV. Carol didn't seem funny to me that evening. When she tugged on her ear to send that secret message to her grandmother, I tugged on mine and prayed that my mother was up in heaven, listening. Then I cried.

Shortly before eight, we left for the service on the beach.

It was a night I'd never forget.

In the gloom of a hidden moon, we strolled down the beach, arm in arm, lost in our grief. My father, my grandparents and me. As we rounded the bend, the Dixon house was ablaze in light from a crackling bonfire that blazed on the sandy beach. Oil lanterns circled widely around the fire pit. The glow from the flickering flames threw sinuous shadows on the side of the house.

Our gaze swept the beach, seeking out the Dixons.

When we saw them, we came to an immediate halt.

There were people everywhere—lined along the beach, hidden by trees and bushes, and camouflaged by gnarled logs and driftwood that separated the grass from the rocks. Indians from town were dressed in ceremonial clothing and their long beaded capes and feathered masks frightened me.

Nana introduced us to *Ta'yii Ha'wilh* Donald Spencer, head chief of the *Huu-ay-aht* people. Chief Spencer had a hawk-like nose and black shoulder-length hair. It was braided and wrapped with strips of hide. He wore a massive headdress covered with eagle feathers and beads.

He shook hands with my father. "I am sorry for your loss."

Then his penetrating black eyes peered into mine. "Welcome, Sarah Richardson, daughter of Daniella Richardson who has gone to the Great Spirit."

He reached out, placed one hand on my shoulder and spoke strange Indian words. Afterward, he turned and welcomed my father in the same way.

"This is all so...wonderful," my grandmother sobbed.

My grandparents were stunned by the warm welcome they received from complete strangers. Over twenty-five people attended. People whom we barely knew surrounded us, and I felt humbled and very grateful.

We were escorted down to the fire and motioned to sit in a circle around it. I sat on a blanket between Nana and Nonna Sofia. Nonno Rocco and my father sat next to my grandmother. Beside them sat Goldie and her parents.

The circle closed and the ceremony began.

WHALE SONG

Tribal dancers in their colorful costumes and intimidating open-mouthed masks stood within the circle around the fire pit. A white-haired elder started beating on a deerskin drum and a younger man joined him with a hand-carved rattle. The drummer began to chant in a raspy voice while the dancers moved in unison as smoke weaved through their writhing bodies.

It seemed more like a dream…ethereal.

Chief Spencer stood up, tall and regal in the firelight, exuding an air of quiet authority. "Welcome," he began. "Today we say goodbye to Daniella Richardson—daughter, wife, mother and friend. She blessed us with her graciousness, rejoiced in the beauty of nature and captured the essence of the Great Spirit in her art." His deep voiced thundered in the night.

The beating of the drum, combined with the chanting voices that surrounded me, lulled me into an odd calm. I relaxed and leaned against Nana.

Suddenly, the singing and drumming stopped.

I looked around me, disoriented, and tasted bitter smoke.

Out of the depths of the lush green forest came a huge, lumbering form. A creature with the body of a man cloaked in black and the head of a wolf stepped toward the circle of light.

I gasped in terror and clung to Nana's arm.

"Don't be afraid, *Hai Nai Yu*," she murmured. "It's the chief's son. He's going to dance a special ceremonial dance about Wolf, the ancient spirit messenger who travels far and wide."

I looked up at her wise face and she patted my hand.

"Wolf is a sage, a powerful spiritual teacher. He talks to the *Spirit World* and will guide your mother there."

Drums and rattles sounded again, beating like a heartbeat.

Puh-pum! Puh-pum! Puh-pum!

Holding my head high, I was determined to be brave while the chief's son danced in the glow of the fire—his wolf mask howling at the invisible moon.

"Wolf medicine is very strong," Chief Spencer said, offering me his hand. "It can heal in ways that the human world cannot."

I stumbled to my feet. My limbs felt tired and weak. The full impact of my mother's death suddenly hit me as I stood in front of the chief, all eyes upon me. My gaze swept across the flames toward the wolf dancer. His wolf mask glared back at me.

I shivered.

"She does not remember," Nana rasped.

Chief Spencer's intense eyes rested on me. "She will. When Wolf walks by her, she will remember…when she is *ready* to see him."

She nodded thoughtfully and smiled at me.

I loved that old Indian woman—regardless of her age, the color of her skin or whether or not we were related. She once told me that we were all connected. Everyone and everything. That night I believed my connection to the people I loved was stronger than a steel rope. And as unbreakable.

When the music stopped, the wolf dancer disappeared into the forest. It was almost as if he'd never existed. I tried to comprehend what the chief had said—that I'd regain my memory when Wolf walked past me. I peered nervously into the bushes, wanting to remember, but mostly afraid to.

My father stood beside me, looking slightly out of place.

Chief Spencer greeted him. "Husband of Daniella, gone to the Great Spirit, we wish you peace. Take comfort in knowing that her spirit lives on—in the earth, trees, wind and water. And in your child." He handed my father a small black pouch. "Hang this in your home as a sign that good spirits are always welcome."

Next, he gave my father a small totem pole carved from red cedar and hand-painted in a natural finish. "The totem represents the importance of family."

He turned to me, his gaze intense. It made me uneasy, until he smiled. "Daughter of the Great Spirit your journey will be long. You must not fear the memories. Your mother's spirit and Wolf will guide you. Take these tokens wherever you go."

He fastened a silver chain around my neck, fastening it gently. Dangling from it was a silver howling wolf pendant.

"The first will guide you on your journey of truth—providing you're brave enough to follow its trail."

He gave me a large gleaming feather. "Eagle's feather is a gift from the creator and most sacred to us. It will help you to seek the wisdom of the Great Spirit. As Eagle soars high, his vision grows—as will your vision."

My last gift was a small totem pole carved from cedar like my father's, and painted with red, black and gold. In the dimness of the night, I examined it, but it wasn't until I heard the chief's words that I understood what I was seeing.

"The Sea Wolf is both whale and wolf, connecting you to land and sea. He will help you find peace, wisdom and unity. He is messenger and guide."

I thanked him quietly and kept the gifts close to me.

The rest of that night passed in a blur. Many of the townspeople had brought dishes of hot food—deliciously seasoned deer stew and casseroles that tasted heavenly. We sat on pieces of driftwood while we ate in the dark.

Just before midnight, moonlight escaped from between the clouds. A beam of light shot through the sky, caressed the ocean and bounced off the restless waves.

Somewhere deep in the woods, a wolf let out an ominous howl. It sent shivers down my spine and I turned to my father for comfort. But instead, I caught Chief Spencer staring at me.

The wolf howled again. *Aaa-ooo...*

And so my journey began.

When I went to bed that night, I carefully placed my precious gifts on the dresser. My grandparents kissed me goodnight, leaving my father and I alone. He sat on the edge of the bed and tucked the blankets around me. Not a word was said.

Then he let out a sigh. "That was a wonderful ceremony."

"Yeah, it was," I said. "Mom would've loved it."

My father stood up, walked to the door. "She certainly would've. I love you, Sarah."

"I love you too, Dad."

Alone, I climbed out of bed and crawled into the window seat. A tear rolled down my cheek. I felt empty.

"Goodnight, Mom," I whispered.

I had disturbing dreams throughout that night, dreams of an eagle swooping down upon me and carrying me off to the den of an ancient silver wolf. Surrounded by murky shadows, I listened for the approaching sounds of my wolf guide and when I heard the patter of paws climbing the rocks below, I held my breath.

A dark shadow lingered in the entrance to the wolf's den. I felt its hot breath at my throat and when I tried to scream no sound came from my mouth. The shape howled mournfully and its hypnotic voice echoed in the darkness.

"Follow me."

Stumbling from my dream-cave, I found myself on a beach. A plaintive cry resounded across the ocean and a plume of sea mist caught my eye. A mama killer whale was skimming the surface, staring at me intently.

"We are all connected," she said.

The wolf-shape beckoned me down a path. "This is the path to the truth."

I took a few steps and stopped. My feet had sunk in the sand and rocks.

"Wait!" I yelled. "I can't move. I'm stuck."

The wolf's yellow eyes sought mine. "Follow my trail...when you're ready."

As the wolf-shape vanished, I thought I heard a melancholy sigh. *Puff...puff.* The eerily familiar sound echoed through the trees.

Then my dream faded into a restless sleep.

112

sixteen

I awoke to the sound of the surf crashing against the shore, and a distant memory of a killer whale surfaced in my mind. I heard birds singing cheerfully outside. When I went to open the window, something caught the corner of my eye. The gifts I had received the night before were gone.

Where are they?

Panicking, I searched the floor and behind the dresser, but my gifts weren't there. I grabbed a pair of jeans and a tattered t-shirt, and was about to throw the shirt over my head when I felt something cold against my chest. My fingers touched the silver necklace hesitantly. *When did I put this on?*

I walked toward my bed to straighten the blanket and it was then that I saw the eagle feather lying on the bedside table, the carved totem pole next to it. Bewildered, I picked up my treasures and placed them back on the dresser.

Wearing the silver necklace, I went downstairs to the dining room. My grandfather was at the table reading the newspaper and drinking strong coffee. Nonna Sofia was making apple pancakes, but I told her I wasn't very hungry.

"*Piccolina*, are you all right?" she asked in dismay.

"I'm tired, that's all." I stifled a yawn. "Where's Dad?"

"He went for a walk on the beach," she replied, expertly flipping the pancakes.

"Nonna Sofia, did you move the things I got last night?"

My grandmother stopped pouring batter into the pan and bustled over to me. "What? Did you lose them?"

I shook my head. "No, I just thought...uh...forget it."

I realized that I must have been sleepwalking. I must have moved everything and placed the necklace around my neck.

Strange.

When we were finished breakfast, my grandfather cleared his throat. "Your dad and I have to make some arrangements today. Your mom's...funeral will be

113

tomorrow."

I nodded mutely.

"Goldie was by earlier," my grandmother said. "She brought you some things from school. Why don't you try to catch up on your schoolwork?"

I gaped at her as if she had gone insane. *School?*

It seemed like years since I had sat at my desk and studied. I felt guilty because my mother had wanted me to have a proper education, but part of me simply didn't care. After all, my mother was gone. Forever.

I wandered out onto the deck, half-listening to the murmurs of my father and grandfather. I stared up at the sky and thought of my mother—her smile and her warmth. I recalled her last days in the hospital and tried to remember what she had whispered to me before going into a coma.

Why can I only see a dark hole when I push myself to remember?

Later that day, while my dad was in town, I overheard my grandparents arguing—something they rarely ever did.

"Rocco," Nonna Sofia said. "He was following her wishes."

"How do we really know those were Daniella's wishes?" my grandfather snapped. "Just because *he* says so?"

"We cannot doubt him, Rocco. He loved Daniella. He would never hurt her on purpose. She made him promise." Her muffled sniffles grew louder.

"Shhh…Sofia, *bella*," he consoled her. "I know…"

I leaned against the wall, listening to their words

"Poor Sarah," my grandmother wailed. "First her mother, now…if Jack goes to prison, I—" She broke into hysterical sobs.

Devastated, I raced upstairs to my room.

I somehow convinced myself that my memory of that day might save my father—that perhaps he had tripped over the cord and maybe my mother's death had been an accident.

If only I could remember.

Gritting my teeth, I mentally walked myself through the moments just before my mother's death. My father and I were alone in her room. I argued with him about something. Then the next thing I knew, I woke up in a hospital bed.

Maybe I saw him do it. Is that why I can't remember?

My memory was blank, like an empty chalkboard. There was nothing I could say to any court judge to make him believe my father was innocent. Nothing I could remember would help him.

My stomach churned.

I crawled into bed and fell asleep holding onto my wolf pendant. If I dreamt at all that night, I don't remember that either.

114

As a compromise to my grandparents, my father arranged a small, informal funeral service in a small chapel in Bamfield. We gathered, united in grief, under a tempestuous sky filled with churning thunderheads. The wind howled through the thin-walled church, causing the stained-glass windows to vibrate as Father Verhagen solemnly welcomed everyone inside.

A blue-robed choir stood to the left of the pulpit, singing a melancholy rendition of *Amazing Grace*, accompanied by an old pipe organ. To the right, a beautiful ceramic urn, hand-painted by a local Indian artist sat on a raised platform, surrounded by flowers and wreaths. A copper-framed photograph of my mother was positioned near the urn.

I plodded up the aisle and stood in front of the urn. Then I reached out and caressed the photo of my mother.

"A handful of ashes," I murmured. "That's all that's left of you." Looking at her filled me with misery and longing.

My father, grandparents and I took our seats in the front row of pews while the Dixon family sat on the opposite side. Behind them, my father's co-workers crowded together, whispering and casting sympathetic glances at my father and me. People from Bamfield, some of whom had attended the beach ceremony, also showed up. I noticed Adam and his family sitting in one of the back pews. Annie was sitting beside him with her aunt. Even Mrs. Higginson and some of my other teachers were there. Mrs. Makowski sat behind me, sniffling into a lacy handkerchief, telling everyone that I had a wonderful future ahead of me—that I was a great artist just like my mother.

Father Verhagen began the service. "We are here to remember Daniella, to celebrate her life and her faith."

I slipped into my own little world, lulled into a sense of security by the priest's words, by his promises that my mother was moving on to a better place and by his certainty that my remaining family would be taken care of.

Tears of sorrow coursed silently down my cheeks. My father squeezed my hand and I held on tightly, refusing to let go. I stared down at our folded hands and wept for my mother.

After the service, we filed out through the double doors of the church and stepped outside. A cold wind flailed at us as we waited at the top of the stairs, sheltered by the porch overhang.

Father Verhagen stopped me. "Your mother is in Heaven, Sarah. God will look after her now."

For some unexplainable reason, his innocent comment made me furious. *"Who will look after me?"* I wanted to demand. But I bit my lip instead and hurried down the stairs, out into the rain.

"Jack Richardson?" a familiar voice called from the crowd.

A tall figure walked toward us.

My heart stopped.

Sgt. Washinski placed a restraining hand on my father's arm.

"I need you to come with me, please?" he said with authority.

Everyone watched in disbelief as a patrol car pulled up beside us, its lights flashing. My father walked passively toward the vehicle, resigned to his fate. He looked over his shoulder and opened his mouth to say something, but immediately closed it and tossed my grandfather his car keys instead.

"Take Sarah home," he told Nonno Rocco.

Sgt. Washinski gave me an apologetic look. Then he turned to my father. "We're placing you under arrest for the second-degree murder of your wife Daniella Richardson."

The crowd gasped in shock.

I was horrified. "Dad, what's going on?"

I tried to run toward him, but Nonno Rocco restrained me. I struggled to get free, hysterically beating my hands against my grandfather's arms. "Daddy!" I screamed.

"You have the right to remain silent," Sgt. Washinski continued, pulling my father arms behind his back. "Anything you say can and will be used against you in a court of law."

Handcuffs encircled my father's wrists and snapped shut.

"You have the right to speak to an attorney and to have an attorney present during any questioning. If you cannot afford a lawyer, one will be provided for you at government expense. Do you understand your rights?"

My father nodded, looking dazed and unsteady as he was escorted into the back seat of the patrol car.

"Wait!" I shrieked. "What about Mom's ashes?"

Sgt. Washinski slammed the car door, climbed in front and drove away. In the backseat window, I saw my father's face pressed to the glass. Then they were gone.

"Your papa will be back," my grandmother said.

"But Nonna Sofia," I wept. "We have to throw Mom's ashes in the ocean."

I clutched her arm—afraid that if I let go, she too would be taken from me.

"Ah, *carina*," she said softly. "We'll do that when your papa comes home."

Nonno Rocco brought my father's car around.

My grandmother climbed into the back seat and patted the space beside her. "Let's go home, Sarah."

I looked over my shoulder at the dispersing crowd. Annie and Goldie sprinted toward me. Behind them, hobbled Nana.

"Are you okay?" Goldie asked me.

"Nothing is okay."

I could barely look at my two friends. My father had been arrested in front of their eyes. Everyone would think that he had murdered my mother. That my father was a murderer.

"Sarah," Annie said. "They must've made a mistake."

Goldie nodded. "We know he didn't do anything wrong. And we know he didn't hurt your mom. He'd never do anything *that* bad."

We formed a circle. With our heads bowed, we held onto each other tightly. *Three Warriors*. As soon as those two words entered my head, a smug voice in my mind whispered, '*Some warrior you are!*' I let go of my friends and took a step back.

Nana beckoned to me. She hunched forward, placing both of her aged hands on my damp face. Then she looked me right in the eye. "Remember, great warriors *never* stop trying."

I blinked, bewildered by her words. Had she read my mind?

For the rest of the day, I thought about her strange comment.

The days flew past, but the nights were endless torture. They were filled with nightmares of death and hopeless despair. At times, I questioned my sanity and whether I would endure. My mother was dead and my father was a murderer.

I thought of him, trapped behind steel bars. His lawyer did his best to get him released on his own recognizance, but bail was denied. The prosecutor thought that my father was a flight risk because he had strong ties to the United States.

Nonno Rocco was adamant that we would stay in the house in Bamfield until the jury released my father. My grandfather drove to Victoria every day that my father's case appeared in court. Sometimes Nonna Sofia would go with him and I would stay at Goldie's house.

Nana visited my house often that winter. She would exchange recipes with my Italian grandmother over a steaming pot of herbal tea. They swapped stories from their childhood and legends from their countries, all the time trying to ignore the terrible things that were happening to our family.

One morning, my grandmother sat down next to me at the dining room table. Nana sat at the other end, waiting patiently.

"You have missed so much school this year," Nonna Sofia said with a sigh. "That is not so good. Your father wants you to go back to school."

I stared at her, open-mouthed. "But—"

"Sarah, your education is very important," my grandmother interjected. "I know it's difficult, especially with your father…away. You will go back after New Years."

Nana nodded in agreement and I felt betrayed, angry.

I stomped outside onto the deck.

I didn't want to go to school. How could I face everyone? The only one I wanted to see was Goldie.

She's the only one who understands.

I peeked in the window and glimpsed my grandmother and Nana talking seriously. Neither of them looked at me, so I darted down the path to the beach. Running along the shore, I headed for Goldie's house. I was halfway there when I stopped. My friend was still in school.

I yanked my bike from behind the trees near the driveway and jumped on it. Then I pedaled down the driveway, not knowing where I was going, not caring. I just knew that I needed to get away, to escape the walls that were closing in around me. I rode down the meandering main road and stopped in front of Adam's house.

I don't know why. I hadn't seen much of him lately.

I leaned my bike against some bushes, brushed the leaves off my sweater, then strolled over to his front yard. The tire swing moved slowly in the soft breeze, calling me and I climbed into it and began pumping my legs. The wind danced through my hair and I closed my eyes, leaning backwards as far as I could go. I felt liberated.

"Hey," someone called.

Startled, I opened my eyes.

Adam stood beside me, watching me thoughtfully.

Embarrassed, I skidded to an abrupt stop. "I, uh…sorry."

"Aw, don't worry about it," he said with a chuckle. "No one uses that old thing much anyway. My mom'll be happy to know *someone* had fun on it today. She keeps threatening to burn it."

"Doesn't your brother use it?" I mumbled.

"Darren? Nope. He wouldn't be caught dead on that thing."

Fascinated by him, I secretly admired his tanned, handsome face, his golden eyes and his quirky smile. All of a sudden, I recalled my first kiss—the moment when his warm lips had touched mine.

I blushed.

We stood in awkward silence, neither of us knowing what to say. The only sounds were the wind whistling through the trees and a wind chime tinkling nearby.

Adam's expression softened. "I'm sorry—"

"I just wanted—" I said at the same time.

He laughed, his golden eyes twinkling. "You first."

"Thanks for coming to my mom's funeral."

"You're welcome."

I gave him a hesitant look. "I was curious why you weren't at the beach ceremony." I shrugged, as if it didn't matter to me.

Adam kicked at a small rock in the grass, shooting it under some bushes. "I had to go to the mainland with my parents and we left the day before your mom…died. We just got back a few days ago." He looked up at me. "I'm really sorry about your mom. Your dad too."

He stepped behind me, grabbed the swing ropes and pulled them toward him. I held my breath. Then he let go. We remained like that for some time—me stuffed into that old tire swing and him pushing me.

I learned that he'd been born in Petawawa, Ontario. His parents had met on the Queen Charlotte Islands. His mother was a Haida Indian and his father had been in the Canadian Armed Forces, stationed at the base in Masset when they'd met and married. After a posting to Ontario, Adam's father resigned from the military and they moved to Bamfield.

"And here I am," Adam said. "What about you?"

I described my experiences growing up in Wyoming, the grassy plains and mountains, the long bus ride to the school in Buffalo and the Shoshone man who had lived in our barn. I told him about Amber-Lynn. She still wrote to me occasionally, but mostly that friendship had faded. I admitted to him that I felt guilty about leaving her behind.

"Sometimes change is good," he said. "Sometimes you just need to move on, maybe to better things."

I giggled. "Jeez, Adam, now you really sound like an Indian."

Behind me, he grew quiet. For a moment, I wondered if I had hurt his feelings and I almost apologized.

He turned the swing so that I faced him. "One day, Sarah Richardson, I'm going to marry you."

I gasped, flustered by the intensity of my emotions. Then I looked away. "I'd better get home."

Ungracefully, I tried to extract myself from the swing, but it spun around, making me dizzy. My legs were tangled and I had to lean on Adam to keep my balance. I fought the urge to giggle and tried to maintain my dignity. But with my arms wrapped around his neck while I hopped on one foot and my other leg sprawled in a tire, it was next to impossible.

A flicker of movement caught my eye.

I saw Adam's mother poke her head out the kitchen window. She seemed startled to see her son holding onto a girl who was balanced precariously on one foot while trying to extract the other leg from the tire. She smiled and quickly ducked inside the house. I swear I saw the kitchen curtain move afterwards.

WHALE SONG

Pedaling home, I was mortified that Adam and I were in such close contact and that his mother had seen us. Yet I was ecstatic that he really seemed to like me. I didn't know if I should laugh or cry. So I did both. I giggled, grinned and wiped my eyes. I was in a state of almost manic euphoria. Every now and then, I would think of his words, stop my bike in the middle of the road and gasp in disbelief. I didn't know what to think.

Adam wants to marry me?

Suddenly, something darted out from the woods.

Jamming on the brakes, I screeched to a stop and almost toppled from my bike. At first I thought it was a shaggy dog that stood in the middle of the road—until I saw the wild intensity in the creature's yellow eyes.

I sucked in a breath and stood silent, motionless…waiting.

A gray wolf had just crossed my path.

seventeen

The wolf stared at me hungrily. It was massive, its coat dark gray with streaks of black. Its eyes burned into my soul and I saw sharp teeth and a panting tongue.

Go away!

The animal took a few steps forward.

A memory flashed and I heard Chief Spencer's prophetic words. *"When Wolf walks by her, she will remember…when she is ready to see him."*

"But I'm not ready!" I shouted at the wolf.

I held my breath.

The wolf's ears perked. Then it vanished.

I remained glued to the road, unable to move. An insistent blast of a car horn sounded behind me and I darted a look over my shoulder. My father's car was heading straight for me.

I dodged to the side of the road, dragging my bike with me. I watched the car slowly back up. Then a furious face glared at me.

"Sarah!" Nonno Rocco yelled. "What on earth are you doing in the road? I almost ran you over."

As he scrambled out of the car, my body began to shake.

"Are you okay, *carina*?" He held my arms and examined me with concerned eyes. "Are you hurt?"

"No. I'm not hurt, Nonno. I'm fine."

With a frown, he tossed my bike into the trunk and we drove away. I couldn't resist glancing over my shoulder. The bushes rustled—as if something hid within. But there was no sign of the wolf.

The following morning, I was half-convinced that I'd dreamt the entire episode. The ghost-wolf, I determined, had been a figment of my imagination.

Christmas came and went, barely noticed in all the confusion and sadness.

121

WHALE SONG

We all agreed that we'd celebrate the following year—when all of us, including my father, would be together. I spent most of the Christmas holidays with Goldie and Annie.

That's when I told them about the wolf.

"Really?" Goldie asked with fearful eyes. "You saw a wolf?"

Annie was so spooked by my story that she phoned me later that night to tell me that she was sure the wolf had followed her home from my house. Of course, she didn't *see* anything.

"But I know it was that wolf," she said.

The next day, I bundled up in a warm jacket and searched the bushes around my house. I looked for wolf prints in the dirt, but I didn't find anything. Not one single paw print.

Heaving a sigh, I darted back into my house. Nonna Sofia was watering the plants, lost in her thoughts.

"Can I go to Goldie's house?" I asked.

She looked up and smiled. "Be back by suppertime."

I gave Goldie a quick call and we agreed to meet by the boat dock. When I passed the bend in the shore, I saw her sitting cross-legged at the end of the dock. She was staring across the bay, one hand raised to shield her eyes from the sun.

"What are you looking at?" I asked when I reached her side.

"Over there." She pointed.

I plopped down beside her and squinted as a ray of sunlight reflected off the mirror-smooth water. "What? I don't see—"

Then I saw it.

Near the shores of Fallen Island, a black dorsal fin emerged.

"My brother has come to visit," Goldie murmured.

We watched as the killer whale crested and leapt out of the water. It crashed down on one side, creating a wall of seawater that was suspended in the air for a second.

"How do you know that's Robert?" I asked.

She pointed again. "See that mark on his back?"

When I saw a white splotch near the whale's fluke, I nodded.

"That's how I know. He has a birthmark on his lower back."

I watched the whale frolic in the bay. "Remember when you first told me Robert was a whale?"

"Yeah," she snorted. "You must've thought I was crazy."

I rolled my eyes. "Absolutely wack—"

"Look, Sarah!" Goldie jumped to her feet.

I stared in amazement as a second killer whale spouted nearby. The whales swam side-by-side before plunging into the ocean depths and disappearing.

Goldie gaped at me. "Two whales in the bay at the same time? I've *never* seen that."

"So, is that your brother's girlfriend?" I asked with a smirk.

"Maybe." Her eyes grew cloudy. "Or…"

Grinning, I rose to my feet. "Or…what?"

When she spoke, her words were seriously quiet. "Maybe that was your mother, Sarah. Maybe she's come to see you."

My heart skipped a beat at her suggestion.

That night, I curled up in the window seat and tried to pick out objects in the shadows around the house. The shed, the stack of firewood…my bike. Then my eyes wandered toward the line of tall cedar and lofty spruce trees. They touched the sky—a hundred soldiers guarding my castle keep.

I glanced toward the ocean. As moonlight bounced off the undulating waves, I thought about the whales in the bay. Was the second one my mother? If so, would she visit me again?

My throat ached and my eyes burned.

I placed one hand flat against the window, its surface cold and hard. "Mom, are you out there?" I leaned closer and my gaze shifted to the bushes below.

Glowing golden eyes glared back at me

I jumped, snatching my hand away.

A gray wolf slinked out from the dense undergrowth. It paused beneath my window and peered up at me.

Aa-oooo…

I scurried from the window seat and held my breath.

The wolf's wistful howl cut through the air again.

Shivering, I slid into bed and tried to ignore my racing heart.

In January of 1980, I returned to school amidst a combination of rumors and sympathy. Mrs. Makowski took me under her wing, encouraging me to create more posters for the school. My *Romeo & Juliet* poster had been well received and in a few weeks the grade one students were going to present the next play—*Little Red Riding Hood*.

I threw myself into my art. My grandparents saw me only at mealtimes and I know they were worried about me.

"Really, Nonna Sofia," I said one afternoon. "Making these school posters makes me feel better. Then I don't have to think of Dad's court case so much."

Nonna Sofia brushed my hair with her fingers. "You're right, *piccolina*. We need to keep busy."

I spent long days working on that poster. I drafted in the background with

123

lush trees and flowers. Red Riding Hood followed a rocky path, carrying her basket full of treats.

There was only one problem.

Every time I tried to draw the wolf, my hands shook.

"This is silly," I muttered after erasing the wolf for the millionth time. Taking a deep breath, I pushed away all negative thoughts and focused on the things I'd learned from Chief Spencer.

Wolf is a messenger who talks to the spirits.

I started on the wolf's eyes, wanting them to be cute and wide-eyed. But when I looked at the finished product, he was licking his drooling chops and eyeing Red Riding Hood hungrily.

I showed Mrs. Makowski my rough draft.

"Can you change his expression just a bit," my teacher asked. "You'll scare all the little ones." She laughed. "He's very realistic, that wolf."

"He's real to me," I muttered.

I carefully altered the poster and eventually got it to my liking. I painted it with my mother's watercolors. When it was finished, the wolf had eyes that twinkled merrily—an intense golden color.

I thought of Chief Spencer's warning.

When Wolf walks by her....

Bold headlines in the *Bamfield Examiner* sensationalized my father's trial. *'Richardson Pulls the Plug Out of Love.'* His was the most controversial case the small town had seen in years. Every time I turned on the TV, I'd see a serious rookie reporter standing outside the Victoria courthouse, revealing some aspect of the trial.

Some people supported my father, saying that he acted out of love and couldn't bear to see my mother suffer any longer. They called him merciful. Others said he had ruthlessly taken my mother's life—a life that only God could take. They labeled him *murderer.*

In February, the day arrived that we had all hoped would never come—the day that I was to testify. Although a wife couldn't testify against her husband, a child could—especially one who had witnessed a crime. But my father's lawyer didn't want me on the witness stand.

"You're useless to me unless you remember something that'll help your dad," Mr. Gregory said in a kind voice.

However, the prosecutor wasn't as kind. He was hoping that I would remember enough to make my father look guilty. That dreaded day, I anxiously took the stand and with one hand on a black Bible, I promised to tell the truth. It seemed like such an easy, simple thing—until the prosecutor began cross-examining me.

He was a burly, gray-haired man in his fifties, intimidating in size and demeanor. And he didn't waste any time getting to the point. "Sarah, you were with your father the day your mother died. Is that correct?"

I nodded.

"Please answer out loud."

"Y-yes," I said in a small voice.

He approached me, placing his hands on the rail in front of me, effectively blocking my view. "At one time were you left alone with your father, in your mother's room?"

"Yes, sir," I said a little louder.

He slid his glasses to the tip of his nose and peered down at me. "What happened next?"

I hesitated for a moment. "I don't remember."

"Did you leave the room?"

"I...don't know." I was distracted by my father who was anxiously whispering to his lawyer.

"Is it true that your father turned off the heart monitor first?"

A memory flashed in my mind. The heart monitor. *Puh-pum.*

I swear I heard a heartbeat. I shook my pounding head, desperate to clear my thoughts. My stomach heaved and I thought I was going to throw up.

The prosecutor turned to the jury. "And that your father proceeded to shut off the life support machines—including the respirator—against Dr. Michaels' orders?"

I envisioned the respirator pumping oxygen into my mother's lungs. *Puff! Puff!* I could almost see my mother's chest buckling, gasping for air. I could faintly recall the colored buttons on the machines, especially the glowing yellow ones.

The prosecutor thumped one hand on the rail. "Answer the question, please."

I glanced from the kind-looking judge in his regal robes to the man in the suit in front of me. "Sorry, what did you say?"

"Did your father shut off all the machines?"

Hot bile rose in my throat. "I don't know. I don't remember."

He glared at me. "Oh, come on. You were right there in the room."

"Objection!" Mr. Gregory yelled, coming to my rescue. "He's badgering the witness. The child's doctor has already confirmed that Sarah Richardson has hysterical amnesia. It's brought on by extreme trauma." He eyed the prosecutor and frowned. "Sarah may not have been in the room She's telling you what she knows. She can't remember."

"Is there any reason to question this witness any further?" the judge asked the prosecutor.

The man pursed his lips. "No, none at all."

"You may step down, Miss Richardson," the judge said in a gentle voice.

My legs were numb and tingling as I walked past my father. He started to rise but his lawyer pulled at his sleeve. Pushing past the small gate, I returned to the seat beside my grandmother. The rest of the afternoon was a blur.

Later, I visited with my father and Mr. Gregory in one of the waiting areas. Everyone was tense and exhausted.

"You did great, honey," my father said tiredly. He looked older with every passing day. "I'll see you soon."

After a round of hugs, he was escorted away by a guard.

On the last day of my father's court case, my grandmother cried softly, praying on a rosary during the entire drive to Victoria.

When we reached the courthouse, Nonno Rocco parked the car and we walked up the steps. Inside, photographers snapped our pictures while reporters shoved microphones into our faces.

"How do you feel knowing that your son-in-law murdered your daughter?" one man asked.

"Get those out of the way," my grandfather growled.

He stared at me, his eyes welling with compassion, and Nonna Sofia hugged me close, shielding me from the voracious claws of the paparazzi. I knew that my grandparents hated what the publicity was doing to me—to all of us.

"Mr. Rossetti!" someone yelled. "Do you believe your son-in-law killed your daughter?"

My grandfather spun on one heel. "Leave us alone."

Mr. Gregory appeared in a doorway. "Mr. Rossetti? Jack wants to speak to you." He escorted Nonno Rocco inside and closed the door, leaving Nonna Sofia and me to wait in a tiny, private room, away from the reporters.

"Nonna Sofia, what's going on?" I asked, biting my lip.

My grandmother sighed. "I don't know, *piccolina*. I'm sure it is nothing."

"Will Daddy be coming home after this?" I asked, holding my breath, afraid of her answer.

She put on a brave face. "I'm sure he will."

But I knew she was lying.

My grandfather stepped into the room. His brows were pinched and his lips thinned as he glanced at Nonna Sofia. He whispered something to her and her face grew alarmed.

Something was wrong.

126

"We must stay here and wait," she said to me. "Only Nonno can go in today."

"Why?" I demanded. "I want to see my dad."

Nonno Rocco leaned forward and gripped me lightly by the shoulders. "You must be brave for your papa. It was his decision that you stay here with your grandmother."

"But I know Daddy would want me there," I argued, holding my head up defiantly. "Why would he want me to stay here?"

Nonno Rocco shook his head sadly. "I'm sorry, but we must trust your father. He's only doing what's best for you."

Someone knocked on the door and a guard escorted us to some chairs just outside the courtroom doors. The reporters had been moved to another part of the building so the hall was quiet.

Nonno Rocco kissed my grandmother and me before walking through the huge double doors. They slammed shut behind him, the boom echoing in the hall long after he was gone.

It felt like we waited for an eternity.

After an hour, I got to my feet and began examining the artwork that graced the hall walls in the old building.

"Nonna Sofia! Look at this painting!"

My grandmother rose to her feet and joined me.

On the wall was a painting by an Indian artist. It showed a ceremonial dance around a campfire. What fascinated me most was the odd figure dancing around the campfire. The dancer was cloaked in a long black cape and he wore a wolf mask. As I stared into his eyes, I thought he oddly resembled Chief Spencer's son—the one who had danced the *Dance of the Wolf.*

A wave of roaring voices erupted from behind the courtroom door. I heard the sound a gavel banging on a solid surface. Suddenly, the door beside us squeaked and swung open. A guard exited. He gave us a brief nod as he passed by. My grandmother and I nervously looked at each other, unaware that the final day of my father's freedom had just arrived.

Mr. Gregory and Nonno Rocco stepped out into the hall. My father's lawyer patted my grandfather on the shoulder and whispered something in his ear. Nonno Rocco looked at Nonna Sofia. When their eyes met, he shook his head very slowly. My grandmother instantly broke into tears.

I waited for my father.

But he never showed.

My grandparents took me aside and broke the news.

After careful deliberation, the jury had found my father guilty of the second-degree murder of my mother, Daniella Andria Rossetti Richardson. He was sentenced to twelve years in Matsqui Institute, a medium-security federal prison on the outskirts of Abbotsford, BC.

I was sentenced to growing up without either of my parents.

PART THREE

Bridge of the Gods

eighteen

After my father's incarceration, I prepared to move to my grandparents' house on the mainland. Nonna Sofia and I packed away all of my parents' belongings. I wrapped my mother's jewelry box with my father's favorite shirt and stuffed it deep into a box filled with clothing and various knick-knacks. We loaded everything—including my things—into a moving van, and I said a tearful goodbye to my beautiful room with the view of the ocean.

Then I walked for the last time on the beach.

"I love you, Mom," I sobbed, tracing the words into the sand with a stick. I circled them with a heart.

I whispered farewell to the sandy beach and wooden raft, then plodded back to the house that was no longer my home. It was time to say goodbye to Goldie and the Dixon family.

They waited in the driveway, their faces painfully sad.

"Don't forget me, Sarah," Goldie said, trying not to cry. She handed me a package. "Open it in the car. It's from all of us."

Nana brushed my bangs from my eyes. "Some day your memories will bring you home, *Hai Nai Yu*. Keep your eyes open for Wolf and don't forget the lesson that Seagull learned."

Sometimes holding onto things only brought suffering.

As we pulled away from *231 Bayview Lane,* I pressed my face against the window. Goldie turned away, sobbing, while her family waved. Nana watched us leave, her long black hair with its unusual white streak blowing in the breeze. I saw her reach a hand upward and pluck something from the sky. She held it high above her head and waved it slowly.

I recognized the object—an eagle's feather.

A minute later, we rounded a curve and they were gone.

With a sniffle, I opened the package that Goldie had given me. I cried out softly at the apparition of a silver wolf. The ornament was about six inches long and shaped from pearlized ceramic.

129

WHALE SONG

I stared at it in dismay.

The wolf strained its head as it voicelessly howled at me.

Follow me!

My grandparents lived in a tiny, crowded two-bedroom condominium in North Vancouver. It was awkward to watch them as they made room for me. Their spare bedroom contained a twin bed and Nonna Sofia's sewing machine, yet within a month they had decorated it in a way that was much more suited to a girl my age.

The high school was a few blocks away and although it was swarming with teenagers, I made very few friends. Rumors preceded me and I was ostracized by my fellow classmates. But that didn't matter to me. I had already begun to disconnect myself from life.

I kept in touch with Annie and Goldie during the first two months, but because they reminded me of melancholy times, I stopped writing and calling. I convinced myself that I was being unselfish by letting their friendship slip away, that they needed to move on without me. Nana frequently stayed with us, hoping to cheer me up with her Indian legends. But I became cynical and short-tempered, and eventually she stopped visiting.

I spent the first year surrounding myself with negative emotions, distrusting anyone who tried to get close to me. I packed away everything that reminded me of my mother and my past life in Bamfield, including the wolf ornament that the Dixons had given me. Every night, I fervently prayed that my amnesia would take away everything—every rotten memory.

My grandparents constantly reminisced about my life in Bamfield. I think they believed it would help to soften me. Nonno Rocco would remind me of the trips on the research schooner with my dad and Nonna Sofia would smile and ask me questions.

"I don't remember," I'd always reply.

I figured if I answered that way often enough, they'd get the hint and leave me alone. I also thought that the more I said those three words, the more real they would become.

My grandparents grew concerned and afraid, so they sent me to counselors, psychologists and even to church. But nothing helped. I didn't want to forgive my mother for dying. And I didn't want to forgive my father for killing her. I internalized my emotions and became increasingly depressed. Especially after my first visit to Matsqui Institute to see my father.

That day, I was filled with apprehension. I'd overheard horror stories from the boys in my class about prison riots and the sexual abuse that inmates were often subjected to. When I entered through the prison gates, I heard them slam and lock with finality.

"Oh God," I moaned, terrified of being trapped inside.

After we walked through a metal detector, my grandmother's purse was searched and we were told to empty our pockets. Then we were led to the visitor's area. I sat down at a table while my grandparents chatted a few feet away with a guard.

The visitor's area was filled with other relatives waiting for their loved ones. When a rough-looking inmate filed past me, I stared at him, terrified. The short, obese black man eyed me indecently and whispered a crude comment as he passed by.

I cringed and looked at the wall. *Hurry up, Dad!*

Then I saw him.

Relieved, I jumped to my feet. "Dad—"

My voice caught in the back of my throat.

My father's closely cropped hair was more gray than blond. His face was gaunt and bruised, and there were dark, puffy circles under his eyes. Although he wore the standard prison uniform, it was obvious that he'd lost weight.

"Hey, Sarah," he said, his voice hoarse.

He hugged me quickly. Then he flicked a self-conscious look at the prison guard. "How's school?"

"Good," I said, not knowing what else to say.

"Are the teachers nice?"

I shrugged. "I guess."

We talked about school, my grandparents, anything except my mother, her death or the fact that my father was in prison for murder. I wanted to ask him what prison was like, but I didn't have the nerve. I don't think I could have handled the truth.

After a few minutes, Nonno Rocco and Nonna Sofia joined us. They talked about inconsequential things. I stared at the floor, lost in my thoughts, and didn't notice when the guard signaled to my father that it was time for him to leave. I felt relieved—thankful that the visit was over. I hated the prison. I hated the bars.

My father wrapped his arms around me, leaned close to my ear. "Do you remember anything yet?"

I shook my head.

When I stepped outside the prison walls, I groaned with relief and breathed in fresh air. I told myself that I'd never go back, no matter what. But my father begged me to see him, and I did.

After the second visit, I hid in my bedroom, pulled out my art books and furiously began my own form of therapy. I drew. I produced pictures of horrible things—demons sent to destroy me, creatures from the sea, anything to vent my anger. Upon seeing my works of art, the psychologist told my grandparents that visiting my father had done me more harm than good. The visits stopped.

In November of 1980, I implored my grandparents to bring me back to Matsqui Institute. I missed my father. For some reason, Nonno Rocco wouldn't look me in the eye. He tried to convince me that visiting hours had been cut back, that it wasn't the right time or that my father couldn't have visitors that day.

Finally, in February '81, I visited my father for the third time. Some of the inmates who walked past me were even seedier than the last time I'd been there. And some looked like normal, law-abiding men—the kind you'd meet anywhere. There was, however, a definite undercurrent running through the prison. I felt it in the unusual restlessness amongst the prisoners.

Even my father appeared agitated.

"Is everything okay?" I asked stiffly. "You need anything?"

He shook his head. "No, I'm good."

We stumbled through an awkward game of *'catch up'*. Neither of us had anything important to say. We'd both shut down.

I couldn't wait for the visit to be over and I glanced at my watch uneasily. When our time was up, I rushed outside. I stood in the rain, lifted my face, and cleansed my soul.

In early June, I flicked on the television during a break from studying and caught a news report that made my heart stop.

Matsqui Institute was on fire.

I ran into the kitchen. "Nonna!"

"What is it?" my grandmother cried out, alarmed. "What's wrong, *carina?*"

We watched in horror as reporters commented on a prison riot while camera footage showed flames engulfing several of the prison buildings.

"Over three hundred inmates have seized control of Matsqui Institute," a reporter stated. "Eight staff members are fighting for their lives on the roof of one of the burning buildings. Rescue teams are now on their way."

The camera panned over to the eight trapped men. They waved frantically at a helicopter hovering above them. The men were airlifted from the building minutes before it collapsed.

"What about Dad?" I asked fearfully.

My grandmother rushed to the phone. I heard her speaking to my grandfather in Italian. I couldn't understand a word, but the sound of someone sobbing translates in any language.

"Nonno will call us back," she reassured me when she had hung up the phone.

We sat at the kitchen table, waiting, daring the phone to ring.

Half an hour later, Nonno Rocco called. My grandmother murmured a few words before passing me the phone.

"Sarah, your papa is fine," my grandfather said.

His voice sounded tinny through the phone receiver.

"Did he get hurt?" I asked anxiously.

"He's a little bruised and sore. He got trampled in the riot but…he's okay."

I sniffled. "Can I see him?"

The line was muffled. "I'm sorry, *carina*," Nonno Rocco said a minute later. "They have to fix the prison before visitors can come back."

My grandmother hugged me after I hung up. "Don't you worry. You'll see your papa soon."

Once more, I threw myself into my art. I painted and designed posters for imaginary plays. Anything to help me escape from the reality that was my life. When kids at school asked about my parents, I lied. I told them that my mother was a famous artist who toured the world and that my father traveled with her. No one really believed me.

I wrote my father every day, sometimes more than five pages detailing my day. But everything I told him was a lie. Except that I wanted him to come home. Every day after school, I waited by the phone, praying that he'd call me. The phone calls became less frequent.

I did what I could to help my grandparents. But mostly, I just stayed out of their way. I knew that they loved me, but I often wondered whether I was a burden to them. At times, their modest home felt claustrophobic and I'd escape outside. I wandered the streets, leaving Nonna Sofia and Nonno Rocco to worry about me.

Three years after I moved in with my grandparents, my father called me. Usually he'd speak to Nonno Rocco, so I knew immediately that something was up.

"Sarah?" he said. "Can you come visit me tomorrow?"

I was relieved that I was finally going to see him, since all of my requests had been denied for one reason or another. In the back of my mind, I sensed that he had something urgent and important to tell me. When I saw him, he looked uncomfortable and nervous.

"I don't want you to come here anymore," he said softly. "Or ask to come here anymore."

I gaped at him, shocked. "But Dad, you're all I have."

"I'll still write and call you occasionally. You need to move forward with your life."

I shook my head. "How can I move forward without you?"

133

"Your grandmother told me that you refuse to go out with your friends, that you no longer call Goldie or even Amber-Lynn. She said all you do is write to me, draw horrible pictures and wait by the phone for me to call."

"What business is it of hers?" I snapped.

"She's concerned about you, Sarah. So am I."

"Yeah, right," I muttered.

He stretched one hand across the table. "You can't lose yourself in school and work. There's more to life than that. It's not *you*."

I scowled at him and yanked my hand away. "How do you know who I am? You're in here. I'm out there, trying to—"

"I know, Sarah. You're trying to live without a mother *and* a father. I'm so sorry for that. Nobody expected that I'd end up here. I just want you to be happy, to find someone you can love."

"Love?" I said, mocking him. "Like you loved Mom—or me? You loved her so much you killed her."

He flinched as if I had slapped him.

All the anger and resentment I had toward him boiled over. Unleashing a tirade of angry words, I poured out everything I had always been afraid to say.

"You loved me so much that you left me alone, with everyone knowing that my father is a murderer. Do you think I want or need *that* in my life? That's fine, Dad. I'll leave. I know when I'm not wanted."

His face drained of all color. "But, Sarah—"

"What?" My eyes blazed with fury. "At least I had Nonno Rocco and Nonna Sofia? Yes, they've been wonderful—everything I could have hoped for. But it's not the same."

I flew out of the chair and stomped toward the door.

"I can't understand what you did," I said, refusing to look at him. "Your lawyer might want to call it suicide, but everyone else calls it murder. I'll never forgive you for killing Mom. She might have begged you to do it, but you should have said *no*." I glared at him. "Don't worry, Dad. I won't be back. Ever!"

Visiting hour was over.

I lived in my grandparents' condo until shortly after my eighteenth birthday. Nonno Rocco had been hinting that they wanted to return to Italy, to the valley near Magione where the Rossetti family had lived for centuries. Nonna Sofia was torn between longing to move and wanting to keep me under her wing. When I assured her that I would survive on my own, my grandparents sold their condo, relocated to Italy and I started a new chapter in my life.

During the following years, I completed university and went on to a career in graphic design and advertising. Those few years of designing posters for school plays had left me yearning for approval and acceptance, so I joined a Vancouver company called *Vision-Quest Advertising*. I worked downtown in a cozy office on the fifth floor, in the design and graphics department. My specialty was creating logos and unique ad campaigns.

I was unmarried, unmotivated and unhappy. My life revolved around designing other people's dreams and fighting off the occasional glimpse of a predatory gray wolf. It was strange how that wolf seemed to follow me everywhere I went.

When my grandparents had packed up my belongings from the house in Bamfield, the boxes had been stowed away in a rental storage unit. There was no room in the condo. Years later, those same boxes were stored in the basement of the small house I was renting in Vancouver. The three gifts that Chief Spencer had given me were safely packed in a shoebox in the back of my bedroom closet.

Sometimes I heard them calling me in the dark, lonely night.

I struggled to come to terms with my feelings toward my father, but the more I thought of him and his role in my mother's death, the more unforgiving I became. I blamed him for leaving me. It was *his* fault that I couldn't get close to anyone or commit to a relationship.

Why should I? Everyone I love leaves me in the end.

My life was filled with monotony—work, home, work. My co-workers tried on numerous occasions to encourage me to go out with them, but I had no interest in developing any relationships with them outside of the office.

After a while, I was able to push Bamfield and my parents from my mind. It was almost as if everything had happened to someone else. There were no constant reminders of my past, so I buried it deep in my subconscious mind. I was an orphan.

nineteen

Two weeks before my twenty-fourth birthday, I picked up the phone and heard a voice I hadn't heard in years. Goldie's.

"Sarah, Nana's in the hospital." Her voice trembled. "In Victoria. She was hit by a drunk driver."

"I'll be on the next plane," I said before I hung up.

Two hours later, I found myself flying back to the island I hadn't seen in more than a decade. Taking a taxi to the hospital, I stared out the window. The streets were still familiar. I arrived at the Royal Jubilee Hospital, paid the taxi driver and got out.

Then I strode into the hospital, remembering the last time I'd been there. *The day Mom died.* I rushed to the information desk and was directed to the third floor intensive care unit. A nurse gave me the room number and I tiptoed inside.

At first, I thought the room was empty. Then I saw her.

Nana was sleeping in the bed by the window. Her head was swollen and discolored, and a large bandage covered one cheek. What frightened me most was that the old native woman's eyes were swaddled in strips of cloth. Blood seeped out one corner.

With a shudder, I turned to leave.

"Hai Nai Yu?"

Startled, I hurried over to her. "Nana? Are you awake?"

I saw the snow-white streak in her hair bob up and down.

"I'm here," I said.

Nana weakly lifted her hand. "You came home." Her voice was raspy but firm.

"Yeah, I did," I said sheepishly. "Goldie told me about your accident. Did you really think I wouldn't come?" I didn't wait for an answer. "Nana, with all those bandages on your eyes, how'd you know it was *me*?"

She smiled in the dim light. "I may have lost my eyesight, *Hai Nai Yu*...but

136

I have not lost my vision."

Then she asked me about my father.

"We're...estranged," I said in a quiet voice.

The old woman shook her head. "It will pass."

I didn't believe her.

"Did I tell you the story of *The Bridge of the Gods*?" she asked.

"Not yet," I said with a smile.

Long ago, the Great Spirit gave the people of the land everything they needed. No one was cold or hungry. But soon two brothers began to argue over the land. The Great Spirit told the brothers to shoot an arrow in opposite directions.

"Wherever your arrow falls, that will be your land."

One brother aimed his arrow high and shot it southwards into the valley. The other brother shot his arrow north into the Klickitat country.

Then the Great Spirit built a bridge over the river that divided the brothers' lands.

"This will connect you," the Great Spirit said. "It will be a sign of peace, so that you and your people may visit those on the other side. As long as you remain friends, the Bridge of the Gods will remain."

For years, the two brothers remained peaceful. But gradually, they became selfish, greedy and wicked. The Great Spirit punished them by withholding the sun's warmth. Soon, the rains came and the people were very cold.

They begged the Great Spirit, "Give us fire or we will die!"

There was an old woman on one side of the bridge who still had some fire left in her lodge. The Great Spirit, softened by the people's pleas for warmth, asked the woman, "What do you want most, in exchange for sharing your fire?"

The old woman asked to be young again.

She shared her fire and the following morning Loo-wit, the old woman, was both young and beautiful. Two young chiefs, one from the south and one from the north, saw the beautiful young woman and fell in love with her.

Loo-wit was charmed by both men and could not decide which she preferred. The men grew jealous of each other, causing quarreling amongst their two tribes. There was much fighting on both sides of the river and many warriors died.

Finally, the Great Spirit grew angry with the people and tore down the Bridge of the Gods, the sign of peace between the two tribes. The Great Spirit threw the rocks from the bridge into the river and turned the two chiefs into mountain peaks. Loo-wit was changed into a snow-capped peak so that neither chief could have her. And the Bridge of the Gods crumbled into the river, its

WHALE SONG

beauty and promise lost in the unforgiving ways of the people.

Nana beckoned me closer. "Anger and resentment can destroy even that which the Great Spirit has created, *Hai Nai Yu.*"

Goldie joined me that afternoon in the hospital cafeteria.

"How did you know where I was?" I asked.

She shrugged. "Nana knew. She's always known, Sarah."

I discovered that before moving to Italy, Nonna Sofia had called Nana and given her the address of my first apartment. From that moment on, the old native woman had kept a watchful eye on me. Whenever I wrote to Nonna Sofia, my grandmother would immediately call Nana.

I couldn't help but laugh. "What a pair."

"They're two of a kind, our grandmothers," Goldie agreed.

The next thing we knew, we were howling with laughter. People stared at us as if we had lost our minds. As we wiped our tearing eyes on our shirtsleeves, I stared at her. It was as if we'd never been apart.

"So what's new with you?" I asked.

I was surprised by the changes in her life. I discovered that she was engaged to a local native artist. Nelson Fergis specialized in carving huge twenty-foot totems. It made me remember my small hand-painted totem pole stored in the shoebox in my closet.

I left Nana and Goldie that evening, promising that I'd return the following morning. Goldie looked surprised when I told her I was staying at a hotel in Victoria until Nana was released from the hospital.

"Can you do that, Sarah?" she asked. "I mean with your job?"

I chuckled wryly. "I haven't taken a holiday since I started there. They owe me."

Nana's fractured ribs mended quickly while the dark bruises covering her body slowly faded. But when the doctor removed the cloth from her eyes two days later, her sight was gone. The doctor suggested that she undergo an operation to try to restore some of her vision.

"I'm too old for operations," Nana muttered, refusing to consider it. "I can see everything I need to. Right here." She pointed to her head.

Goldie and I became absorbed in renewing our friendship and I never realized until that moment how much I had missed her. I missed sharing my thoughts with someone. We walked around Victoria, arm in arm, giggling like teenagers and ignoring the odd looks that we received.

"You ever hear from Annie?" I asked, curious.

"Yeah, she's in Ethiopia now."

I stared at her, stunned. "What the hell is she doing there?"

"She's building wells." She giggled.

"What do you mean, building wells?"

"She married a Presbyterian minister. They have two children, both boys. They're living in Ethiopia, building drinking wells in some of the villages."

I was speechless.

Goldie nodded. "I know. Who would've ever thought, huh?"

"Yeah," I agreed.

We sat by the water fountain in the park across from the hospital and watched a group of young Sea Cadets. They were playing baseball. Two Cadet instructors—one wearing a purple shirt—had their backs to me. They were busily instructing the children in the rules of the game. One team wore black and silver jerseys while the other wore green and blue.

The innocent, carefree laughter of the children mesmerized me, as did the lean form of one of the men—the instructor of the black team. I laughed when a baseball rolled toward us and stopped a few feet away. The child in me wanted to get up, grab the ball and pitch it across the field. But that child was gone.

"What about you, Sarah?" Goldie asked, interrupting my thoughts. "How's your dad doing?"

I shook my head, the smile fading from my face. "I haven't seen him in years."

She eyed me, curious. "Don't you visit him?"

"No," I said firmly. "He asked me to stop visiting a long time ago." I left it at that, hoping that she wouldn't persist.

If she *was* about to say something, she was interrupted by a loud shout from the field. The group of Sea Cadets cheered as one small boy ran around all the bases. He skidded to a stop past home plate. The black and silver team had won.

The Cadet instructor in the purple shirt high-fived his team, gathered up the baseball bats and motioned for the kids to pick up the stray balls. A short, stocky boy left the group and ran toward us. As he leaned down to pick up the baseball, he glanced up at me and smiled sweetly.

I waved to him, but when I noticed his jersey logo, I froze.

Sidney Sea Wolves.

A vision of yellow eyes flashed in my head.

"Wolves," I mumbled, my mouth suddenly dry.

The boy's smile faded and he eyed me guardedly. Then he darted away, his shoes kicking up dust. I have no idea what he thought when he heard that one word, but I do know one thing. I had frightened him.

Squinting into the sunlight, I watched as he approached the well-built man in the purple shirt. The boy whispered something in the Cadet instructor's ear. The man draped a comforting arm around the boy's shoulder, then hastily glanced my way.

I couldn't see him clearly, but I knew that he wasn't pleased.

Nana recuperated from the car accident, stubbornly refusing to use any topical medicines except her native remedies. Oddly enough, her cuts healed without leaving a scar. Even the doctors were amazed.

Determined to get back to work, I returned to Vancouver a week later—much to Goldie's dismay. I was just finishing an ad campaign for a new nightclub in Burnaby when the phone rang.

"Sarah?"

It was my father.

"What do you want, Dad?" I asked stiffly.

"I...I'm getting out next month," he said in a hesitant voice. "They're letting me out on early parole. I'd like to see you, Sarah. Before I get out. I...miss you." His voice sounded old and rough, but his words sounded sincere.

They stirred my guilt. I'd spent years carefully warehousing my emotions, stowing them in the dark recesses of my mind.

Now my father was back. And he was opening *Pandora's Box*.

I let out a weary sigh. "Dad, I, uh—"

The door to my office was flung open and my heavily scented supervisor tiptoed in. He grinned and gave me an exaggerated bow. William West—a.k.a. *Willie* to everyone who knew him—was a colorful character given to flamboyant fashion and dramatic entrances.

"Sarah!" he hissed.

I pointed to the phone and mouthed, *"I'm busy."*

Willy uttered a contrite gasp, then sidled closer to my desk.

"Sarah, are you there?" my father said.

"I can't talk right now," I muttered into the receiver. "When will you be—" I flicked a look at Willie. "Out?"

I jotted the information down on a post-it paper.

"Thanks for calling," I said in a cool tone. "Goodbye."

My father was still talking when I hung up.

Willie grinned. "I'm sorry, hon. Did I interrupt something?"

"No. Nothing important." My eyes narrowed. "Why, what do you want?"

"Is that any way to treat your boss?" He stroked his freckled face thoughtfully. "How's the restaurant coming?"

I watched him, suspicious. "It's almost done. Why?"

Willie shrugged. "No reason."

He plopped down in the chair across from me, crossed his legs and folded his well-manicured hands neatly in his lap. His closely cropped, fiery-red hair clashed with his impishly effeminate face and when he grinned at me, I knew that the man had something up his sleeve.

I frowned. "Yeah, right. What do you want this time?"

"We have a new client…and he's a real babe." He raised his eyebrows suggestively.

"So what?" I said, uninterested.

"Well, honey, he specifically requested *you*."

I gave him a disdainful look. "Why would he ask for me?"

Willie leaned forward. "I don't know. Why don't you ask him yourself? He's outside in the waiting room. Mr. King already interviewed him. You've been assigned to help him with logos for his team." He stood slowly. "Oh, and honey? Let me know if you'd like some help. He's positively delicious." He drifted out of my office, leaving behind an overwhelming trail of cologne.

I stared at the wall, curious why a potential client would ask for me. After all, I hadn't built up much of a reputation in the advertising world and there were others in my department who created sports logos just as well, if not better than I did.

"What's so special about this new client?" I muttered.

Gathering my courage, I picked up the phone and turned my chair away from the door. "Maura, the new client—what's the guy's name?"

I didn't hear her reply because someone rudely barged into my office.

"Hey, Sarah," a deep voice said behind me.

twenty

My temper flared. I slammed down the phone, bolted to my feet and whipped around to face the intruder.

"Long time no see," Adam Reid said.

So many memories crowded my mind that I stammered my response. "H-hi, Adam. W-what are you doing here?"

"Gee," he said wryly. "If I'd known I'd get this warm a welcome..." He shrugged.

I studied every inch of the man—from his size twelve black dress shoes to his thick chestnut hair flecked with gold. He wore a tailored gray suit that fit his tall, athletic body like a glove. When he smiled again, I noticed that his teeth were perfectly white, perfectly straight. Everything about him was perfect.

I subconsciously wiped invisible drool from my mouth. I was tempted to stand and work off some of the restless energy I felt, yet spellbound by his intense gaze.

One day, Sarah Richardson, I'm going to marry you...

"Have a seat, Adam," he mimicked. "Don't mind if I do."

He made himself at home in a chair, his extraordinary golden eyes casually sweeping down my body.

"You look wonderful," he said.

"So do you," I replied mindlessly. "I mean, uh...you look...older." I twisted uncomfortably and pinched myself under the desk, ordering myself to shut up.

Quit acting like a foolish teenager.

As soon as that thought flickered in my mind, I remembered my first kiss. Adam's kiss. Blushing, I rose to my feet and stood with the desk between us like a barrier. I took a deep breath, reminding myself that I was a professional.

"So what exactly do you want?" I asked calmly.

There was a gleam in his eyes before he answered. "My kids need some t-shirts designed. For their baseball team."

142

His kids? I felt a lump in my throat. *I wonder how many kids he has…probably broods of them.*

"It's too hot for jerseys," he continued. "We want something more visual, something more than just the team name."

I glanced at his left hand and scowled. The man didn't even have the decency to wear his wedding ring.

"Look, Adam," I said, gritting my teeth. "I'm not in the habit of making uniforms for a family sports day. I usually handle corporate clients—not some dad with enough kids to make a baseball team for crying out loud."

He stared at me and chuckled softly.

"What?" I snapped, incensed by his obvious amusement.

"The t-shirts are for my Sea Cadet team—not my own kids. I don't have kids. I'm not even married…yet." He choked off a laugh.

I abruptly closed my mouth, feeling foolish and somewhat relieved by his admission. Embarrassed, I hung my head and tried to sort through my jumbled thoughts.

Treat him like any other client.

"What kind of logo are you looking for?" I asked in an attempt to change the subject. But I realized that he was like no man I'd ever known.

"Have dinner with me," he said smoothly. "To discuss my advertising needs."

I took a deep breath. "What time?"

"I'll pick you up after work."

He sauntered away like something wild, on the prowl.

For the remainder of the afternoon, I was unable to accomplish any work. My mind constantly flickered to my dinner date with Adam.

"It's not a date," I corrected. "It's strictly business."

The restaurant Adam had chosen was *Valencia*—a romantic Italian restaurant on Granville Island that made its own homemade pasta. Soft violin music played in the background, soothing my ruffled nerves. We were seated at a candlelit table on the veranda that overlooked False Creek.

Adam signaled to the waiter. "How about some champagne, Sarah? We can celebrate our new…partnership."

I looked up at him, confused. "Partnership?"

He grinned. "The new t-shirts for my team?"

Blushing, I took a healthy gulp of champagne.

"Tell me about your job," he said.

I shrugged. "It's challenging. Sometimes a client has a specific vision and if we're lucky, we'll see the same thing. What about you?"

"I'm a marine biologist." He stared at me. "Like your father. In fact, it was all those trips with your Dad that did me in. How's he doing anyway? I hear he's getting out this month."

"In two weeks," I said quietly.

I didn't want to discuss my father with anyone—not even with Adam—so I changed the subject abruptly.

"Do you ever go back?"

He nodded. "All the time. I work at the marine station sometimes. Mostly I work in Vancouver though. Don't you miss the Island? We had some great times there. Remember 'Ape Man'?"

"Mr. Foreman—who could forget him? Yeah, those were good times." I sighed wistfully.

The depths of his yellow-gold eyes captured me. Leaning forward, he touched my hand. "I haven't forgotten, you know."

"H-haven't forgotten...what?"

He stared at me for a moment. "Have you ever gone back out, on the water?"

Speechless, I watched his tanned hand caress mine. His thumb lightly traced the underside of my palm.

"You should, you know."

His voice and his touch sent a shiver up my spine.

I yanked my hand away. *He's a client. Nothing more.*

We ate dinner in partial silence, broken only by awkward chitchat. After dessert, I took out my notebook and pen.

"Do you have a name or do you need ideas?" I asked matter-of-factly.

"No, we have a name already," he said. "But we want something more visual. Maybe a graphic with the team name."

"What's the name?"

"The *Sidney Sea Wolves*."

I knocked over my champagne glass. I had seen that name somewhere. *The park!* The day that Goldie and I had visited Nana in the hospital.

Thinking of Nana made me remember something else.

When Wolf walks by her...

"How strange," I murmured.

"Is something wrong?"

"I saw you," I admitted. "At the park last week."

He nodded. "I know."

I looked at him, surprised.

"I saw you sitting by the fountain," he said. "I recognized Goldie, but I wasn't sure if it was really you. So I called her."

I swallowed hard.

Now everything made sense. Adam showing up at the agency—requesting me personally. *But why?*

I was afraid to ask.

After we finished dessert, he drove me back to my tiny bungalow. Unlocking the front door, I nudged it open and started inside. I felt a hand on my arm, detaining me, pulling me back gently.

Adam spun me around to face him and his golden eyes gleamed possessively as he lowered his head. His hand slid under my hair and cradled my face.

Then he kissed me...slowly...seducing my very soul.

It was nothing like the kiss he had given me when we were teenagers. This time, it was full of unleashed passion, hot and yearning. For a second my mind and body responded as if it were the most natural thing to do.

"Do you remember?" he murmured against my lips.

I pulled away, shaking, not wanting to think back to that time. The time when my life was turned upside down. Nothing good could come from remembering. Adam was part of past memories—memories I needed to push aside.

"Do you remember when I first kissed you?" he persisted.

I pushed past him, shaking my head. "No, I don't remember anything." Without looking at him, I closed the door.

"*Sarah?*" he called.

I cursed under my breath.

"*I remember, Sarah.*"

I leaned against the door and pressed a hand to my lips.

"Some things are meant to be forgotten," I whispered.

A hideous two-headed beast from hell was torturing my mother, ripping her to pieces. I reached out to save her, my fingertips grazing hers, but I couldn't grasp her hand. I heard her horrific screams of terror as the creature tried to push her off a rocky ledge.

Sisiutl.

"*Don't look at it!*" *my mother screamed.*

I knew that if I glanced at Sisiutl I would be turned into stone, so I gave my mother my undivided attention. I shrieked in terror as Sisiutl whipped its body at me, hurtling me at my mother's feet. I gazed up into her wolfish eyes and she howled in despair.

Sisiutl slithered closer. "Sssarah. Look at me."

Exhausted and beaten, I surrendered to the beast and stared it in the eye. It held me captive, alone and afraid, in its vicious glance. Then the creature's shape shifted. A man's form emerged.

"Daddy?"

"Sarah, look at me," he commanded in a husky voice.

I saw my father—his familiar face—turn to me. Something long and thin dangled from his hand. He held the remains of Sisiutl's tail. He watched me with a sad expression on his face. Then he whistled and my mother leaped safely from the ledge to the ground below, her body transforming into a silver wolf.

"Are you ready to remember?" the she-wolf asked.

The tail in my father's hand slowly transformed—into a long electrical cord. My father handed it to me and I stared at it.

Panting, my wolf-mother crept closer to me, closer to my father. She peered at me, her wolf eyes begging me to remember.

"Remember..."

A hospital room flashed in my mind. Machines and strange noises invaded my thoughts. The smell of death lingered in the air and I found myself back in my mother's hospital room— a child once more.

My father stood by the door. His angry face made me cringe.

"I promised her, Sarah," he screamed at me. "But I can't let her go! You just don't understand—"

"Of course I understand," I cried. "I love her too!"

I awoke from that dream, sweating profusely. Even my hair was soaked. In my lonely bed, I gasped for air and tried to quiet my racing heart. I didn't sleep for the remainder of the night. Instead, I crawled from my bed, put on a pot of Chai tea and sat in the shadows on the bedroom floor with the shoebox full of memories in front of me.

An hour passed before I finally had the courage to tear the lid off the box. I removed the silver wolf necklace, the eagle feather and the Sea Wolf totem pole that Chief Spencer had given me so many years ago. I recalled everything he had told me that night.

Your mother's spirit and Wolf will guide you.

I reached inside the box and pulled out the whale sculpture that Adam had given me. *To remember your mother,* he had said so long ago.

Next, I removed the wolf statue that Goldie had given me.

Placing my treasures together on a small table, I leaned up against my bed and sighed with resignation. "It's time."

I picked up the wolf pendant and thought of every incident where a wolf had come into my life. How ironic that Adam was the instructor of a team called the *Sydney Sea Wolves.*

I fastened the chain around my neck. Closing my eyes, I thought of the yellow gleam of a wolf's eyes—Adam's eyes.

I heard a drum beating hypnotically. *Puh-pum! Puh-pum!*

Chief Spencer's words echoed in my mind.

When Wolf walks by her, she will remember…

I thought of every wolf I had seen over the years. From the time I'd left Bamfield to that very moment, I had been haunted—*hunted*—by them.

…when she is ready to see him.

"I'm ready now," I sobbed as tears burned down my cheeks.

I cautiously opened the floodgate. At first, the memories approached slowly—like unwelcome visitors. I recalled the day my mother had woken from her coma. I remembered her whispered, desperate plea.

"Let me go, Sarah."

Finally I remembered.

Everything.

twenty-one

Matsqui Institute waited impatiently for me like an old haunt, ravenous for its next sacrifice. It was surrounded by a ghostly mist and looked deathly dreary in the depressing thunderstorm. Its walls were drenched with slick rain, the torrential downpour beating on tinny rooftops like a band of drummers. The gates squeaked open—resisting.

I moved forward, chilled to the bone. Walking down the brightly lit hallway, I passed curious guards escorting sullen inmates back to their cells. I held my head high, but my stomach churned—not in fear but in guilt.

I recalled Nana's wise words. *Forgiveness sets you free.*

When I reached the visitor's area, I sat in a quiet corner, waiting. I gazed directly into the eyes of each inmate. Suspicious of me, they sauntered away like disappointed children.

My father reached the table and I stared at him, taking in every line and wrinkle…every bruise and scar. His gaze met mine and I sensed his uncertainty. I had no idea where to begin.

"I, uh…I'm so happy you're here, Sarah," he said.

A strained silence surrounded us.

"I'd like to know if you'll see me," he said. "When I'm out in two weeks. I'd like to be part of your life again."

So many emotions were trapped in my heart. My eyes burned with unshed tears and I ached to tell him the truth. That I remembered.

"You didn't ask me," I whispered.

My father frowned. "Oh…sorry. Will you let me be part—?"

I shook my head, interrupting him. "No. You didn't ask me if I…remember."

He stared past me and I saw the muscles constricting in his throat. I could almost taste his fear. After a moment, his blue eyes captured mine. They watered as he took a deep breath. "Sar—"

148

"Why?" I demanded, shaking my head slowly.

He reached for my hand. "Because I love you."

"But Dad," I moaned. "All these years—you were innocent."

"I knew that, Sarah. But I had no idea that they'd find me guilty and that I'd end up here. All I could think about was you. Your doctor warned me that forcing your memory would be too dangerous."

I sobbed quietly. "I loved her, you know. I really loved her."

"I know you did, honey."

"I never told you what she said." I swallowed hard. "She said '*Let me go*'."

There was a long silence.

Then my father slumped in his chair. "What exactly do you remember?"

"Everything. Dad...can you ever forgive me?"

"Sarah, honey," he whispered. "I'm the one who needs forgiveness. For not being stronger. For not insisting you visit me...for leaving you alone to cope with it all." A tear slipped from his eye. "Tell me what you remember."

I glared at him. "Mom doesn't want to be stuck on these machines."

My father sighed, his blue eyes flashing at me with frustration. "I'll go to the courthouse and request a removal of all life support."

"But that'll take too long. I can't believe that you don't care what Mom wants."

"Sarah, I can't make that decision. Why can't you understand that? As long as there are signs of life—"

"Life?" I shouted. "You call that life? Look at her—she's already dead."

He gaped at me, then stormed out of the room.

Alone, I felt angry and abandoned. Time moved in slow frames, flickering from past to present. I glanced at my mother's comatose body in the bed and recalled her plea, the words she had said to me before she slipped into the coma.

"Let me go, Sarah. Let me go."

Working myself into a frenzy of despair, I moaned. "Okay, Mom. I'll let you go now. Dad won't do it, but I will."

I pushed away from her and tugged at each cord, each connection—twisting and turning buttons until every machine was inactive. The monitors ceased their incessant noise and their futile attempts to give my mother life.

The room grew deathly still.

"I love you, Mommy," I whispered hoarsely.

With the respirator cord lying lifeless in my hand, I embraced my mother again and felt the last remnants of air escape her lungs. Her eyes were closed and she looked peaceful—an angel without wings. I brushed her hair gently with my fingers, tracing the angles of her face.

One last time I kissed her.

Then I draped myself across her. I stayed like that for a long time, praying for escape. The anguish I felt was so intense that I wanted to die alongside my mother. But instead my mind retreated into a fog.

Suddenly, the door opened.

My father stood paralyzed and speechless, unable to comprehend what I had done. He forced himself toward the bed, calling my name, but I was lost in a fugue-like state. He peeled me away from my mother's lifeless body and gently removed the cord from my hand. He raised his tear-streaked face and his penetrating gaze made me shiver.

"Sarah," he moaned in an anguished voice. "What have you done?"

The horror in his voice made me do the only thing I could.

I ran.

When I finished telling him what I remembered, my father didn't say a word. Instead, he glanced over my shoulder and I saw every emotion cross his face. He had taken a terrible risk and had paid for my actions with almost a decade of his life.

"What now?" I asked apprehensively.

"We go on with our lives."

I glanced at the steel bars in the window. "When the truth comes out will they lock me up?"

He shook his head. "You were a traumatized child back then. Why do you think I didn't say anything all these years? No one needs to know, Sarah."

"But *I* know the truth!"

"The truth doesn't matter now. Except to you and me."

A bouquet of lavender roses had been left on my doorstep. I picked it up and inhaled the fragrant scent. I was about to read the card when I heard the soft scrunch of footsteps in the grass.

"They're from me."

I spun on my heel.

Adam leaned against a tree. "For our one week anniversary."

My breath caught in my throat and before I realized what I was doing, I threw myself into his arms. I felt his heart pounding—beating like a native drum. His lips caressed my hair while his lean body pressed intimately against me.

We stayed like that for a long time.

"Well, well," he said finally. "That's *some* way to greet a guy. You do that to all the guys who come knockin'?"

I laughed and dragged myself away. "Just the cute ones."

Unlocking my front door, I pushed it open and we stepped inside. I dropped my keys on the table by the door, then followed Adam into the living room. He sat on the couch and pulled me down beside him.

"How did it go?" he asked, his voice filled with concern.

"What do you mean?"

"With your dad. I know you visited him today."

I chewed my bottom lip. "How—?"

"Your dad and I've been exchanging letters for the past few years," he said with a chuckle. "He's been a mentor to me. He actually got me the temp job at *Sea Corp*. If I had a question, your father would advise me. In fact, when my boss told me I could name the new schooner, I wrote to your dad to see if he had any suggestions."

I wove my fingers through his. "Did he?"

He nodded. "He suggested a great name. One that reminded him of your mom."

I waited.

When he remained silent, I nudged him. "Well, what is it?"

He spread his arms along the top of the couch, stretching like a wildcat. "You'll just have to wait and see."

Trying not to laugh, I held a pillow above his head. "Tell me."

He pursed his lips and endured a soft thump to the head before grabbing the pillow from my hands. Then he leaned over and kissed me soundly on the lips.

During the next week, I plunged headfirst into waters I had never dared to swim. Never before had I allowed myself to be vulnerable, to love someone openly and honestly. Adam awoke in me feelings that I never knew I had. He was my salvation.

I struggled daily with the guilt that I felt regarding my father. Eventually I realized that he was right. Even if the truth were to come out it would make no difference. We had both suffered and paid—in our own way.

It was time to move on.

On the day of my father's release, Adam drove me to the gates of the prison. I felt apprehensive about my father's future.

What will he do? Where will he live?

Glancing up at the bleak prison walls, I realized that I would never have to lay eyes upon Matsqui Institute again.

Adam squeezed my hand gently. "It's going to be fine."

The old metal gates squealed open and my father stepped out into the sunlight. He looked around uncertainly until he saw us.

WHALE SONG

"Hey," he greeted us, hauling a small suitcase in one hand.

I rushed from the car and gave him a hug.

Adam shook my father's hand. "Nice to see you again, Jack."

I studied my two men for a moment. Then I grabbed the suitcase and threw it into the trunk. Sitting in the back seat, I patted the space beside me and smiled at my father. "Get in."

He hesitated. "Give me a minute."

Under a brilliant blue sky, he closed his eyes, sucked in a breath and stretched his arms to the heavens.

I could only imagine what my father must have felt.

Free at last.

We all were.

My father moved in with me.

"Just until I find an apartment," he said.

On his first second day of freedom, we sifted through the boxes that were stored in my basement. There were numerous cartons containing my parents' belongings.

"When you find your own place," I said. "You can take those with you, Dad."

"You'll want some of your mom's things too."

He rummaged through a large crate and I saw him secretly pocket a few items. I left him in the basement, surrounded by half-opened cartons and bittersweet memories. In the kitchen, I made some strawberry tea and wandered about the house aimlessly.

"Sarah?" My father's voice echoed from the basement.

I heard his footsteps thump up the wooden stairs. When he reached me, he had something in his hands. A painting wrapped in a fragment of old fabric.

"Mom wanted you to have this."

He peeled off the cloth.

The vision of a family of killer whales, swimming in a lush lagoon made my eyes water. A crystal waterfall flowed from the forest above like a silky sheet of satin.

"This was the last painting Mom ever made," my father said softly. "And she painted it for you."

He handed me the painting. "She named it…on the back."

I turned it over and let out a gasp.

152

twenty-two

Whale Song.
For Sarah, with all my love.

I thought of the whale that had saved me, its smooth body nudging me up to the surface for air. I recalled the whale pod frolicking in the bay, their songs of life transmitted through the depths of the ocean.

Whale Song.

I smiled, thinking how appropriate it was. I remembered my mother's smiling face while she listened to the mournful sounds of the killer whales in the bay.

The phone rang, abruptly shattering my thoughts.

It was Adam and he seemed excited.

"Sarah, is your dad there?"

With a shrug, I passed the receiver to my father.

I disappeared into the kitchen while they spoke.

"We still have something we need to do," my father said to me, after hanging up.

He opened a small box that he'd retrieved from the basement.

"Mom's urn!" I cried.

We stared at the urn.

My father bit his lip. "Mom wanted us to—"

"I remember," I interrupted gently. "She wanted us to throw her ashes into the ocean."

He nodded. "Adam's taking us to Bamfield tomorrow."

I placed the urn in the center of the table with my treasures.

"I agree, Dad. It's time to let her go."

After supper, my father and I reminisced long into the night. The journey back to Bamfield rested heavily on our minds. I fell asleep shortly before dawn. I dreamt of the Sea Wolf—both whale and wolf—guiding me home at last.

WHALE SONG

Chirping birds argued outside my window and I groaned. I opened my eyes, blinked at the clock and gasped.

I had slept in.

I jumped out of bed. "Bamfield, here I come."

Stomping downstairs in my bathrobe, I followed the scent of fresh brewed coffee. I made it as far as the living room where I came to an abrupt halt.

I had arranged my precious treasures—the eagle's feather, the Sea Wolf totem, the silver wolf statue and the repaired ornament of the mama whale and her baby on a table in front of the window. But there were some new additions to her memorial table. My father had unearthed the urn containing my mother's ashes. Next to it sat her photograph.

"Mom."

She stared at me—beautiful and alive.

In the window, a small black pouch hung from a string attached to the curtain rod. It was the pouch that Chief Spencer had given my father. *'Hang this in your home as a sign that good spirits are always welcome.'*

I caressed my mother's photo, recalling Nana's wise words from so long ago. *"You have to be willing to release her or she'll be trapped between both worlds, Hai Nai Yu."*

"I let you go, Mom," I whispered. "Now it's your turn."

In the kitchen, I let out a hoot when I found my father dressed in a frilly flour-coated apron, a flipper in one hand. Pancakes were heaped on a plate on the counter and bacon sizzled in a frying pan. He had made breakfast for an army.

He handed me a cup of coffee and a plate. "Eat up, Honey-Bunny. Adam will be here in half an hour."

I dug in, famished and touched by his use of my old nickname. Then I went upstairs to get changed and ready for a day that was long overdue.

When Adam arrived, he shook my father's hand and kissed me lightly on the forehead. I think my father was a bit surprised.

"Uh, Sarah," he murmured as we headed outside. "Are you and Adam, uh...you know."

I grinned and threw an arm around him. "Yeah, we are."

"Are what?" Adam said, holding the car door open for me.

I shook my head, laughing, then climbed into the car.

During the drive to Vancouver Island, I admired my two favorite men. My father had blond hair and intense blue eyes while Adam was tall, tanned, dark-haired and had the most amazing golden eyes I'd ever seen.

My Adam.

My Wolf.

Bamfield hadn't changed much in the past decade. The shop where Goldie's mother had sold her hand-woven baskets had been turned into a small strip-mall, but *Myrtle's Restaurant & Grill* was exactly where we had left it, although the building had expanded. When we drove down the main street, it was as if I were eleven years old again.

"Is our house still the same?" I asked Adam.

He nodded and squeezed my hand. "*Almost* the same."

I pulled down the visor and glanced at my father in the mirror. He sat in the back seat of the vehicle holding a box ain his lap. He was completely immersed in his surroundings…and his thoughts.

I flipped up the visor and left him to his memories.

As we reached *231 Bayview Lane*, the gravel driveway meandered into the trees away from the shoreline. I recalled the feeling of dread, that *knowing* that my life would change the moment we drove into the trees.

My life *had* changed. Forever. *Destiny…*

The house appeared and I let out a gasp.

Our old home had been turned into an art gallery. *Island Arts.*

"Mr. and Mrs. Joseph couldn't bear to live in it afterwards," Adam said softly. "When they came back from Florida, they donated it in honor of your mom."

His quiet explanation made my heart ache. I know my father felt humbled too.

"Let's take a look," he said, his voice thick with emotion.

We climbed out of the car and went inside the gallery.

I immediately recognized the old wood stove and the wooden shelf above it. Only one item from my past remained on that shelf—the eagle's feather. On the wall above it was a small gold plaque, recognizing my mother's life and honoring her as the inspiration for the gallery.

My eyes teared when I read it.

In honor of Daniella Richardson, one of the Great Spirit's own masterpieces, and a life well lived and well loved.

"The schooner's waiting," Adam said after a quick call on his cell phone.

I hovered in the doorway of my old home and felt a draft of air breeze over me. It was warm and comforting.

"It's time to go, Mom," I whispered.

It was a short drive to the docks and when we unfolded ourselves from the car, I closed my eyes and breathed in the familiar scent of saltwater and kelp.

Adam pointed to a magnificent schooner. "There she is."

The boat must have been at least twenty-eight feet long. It was painted sparkling white with brass accents and a gold cedar trim.

"She's lovely," I smiled.

My father tucked the box with my mother's urn under one arm and took my hand, steering me toward the boat. "Did Adam tell you I helped him name this schooner?"

Without waiting for a reply, he practically dragged me down the ramp, toward the schooner.

Helplessly, I glanced back at Adam. "Save me."

Adam grinned. Then he grabbed my other arm and I was carried to the boat, my feet barely grazing the ground.

"Okay, you two," I said suppressing a laugh. "You can put me down now."

Adam pointed toward the back of the schooner and I gasped when I saw the name that my father had suggested.

Whale Song.

Just like my mother's painting.

"It's perfect," I whispered.

We climbed aboard the schooner and Adam introduced us to Max, a friendly Australian skipper from 'down under'. Then he eagerly showed my father the latest state-of-the-art echolocation equipment. Times had changed and the technology had greatly improved since my father's day.

I sat down in a deck chair and listened while Adam explained how the new equipment worked. After a while, their murmuring lulled me into a light sleep.

Whale Song headed out to sea and the gentle tossing of the schooner made me feel alive and carefree. The ocean's surface was dotted with foamy waves while radiant beams of sunlight danced on the water like crystal beads.

I sighed, smiling contentedly when Adam sat down beside me. He pulled me close and I rested my head on his shoulder.

"Why did you agree to name her *'Whale Song'*?" I asked.

"When I spoke to your father a few years ago, he mentioned your mother's painting. The one she painted for you. He said that one day *Whale Song* would be yours." Adam reached down, tugged my chin upward and kissed me. "And I thought that name would be perfect because I knew that one day you'd be mine."

Twenty minutes later, Max cut the engines. Adam tossed a microphone overboard and cranked up the volume. We listened for almost half an hour, but all we heard were noisy fish.

"The whales haven't been coming in this close lately," Adam apologized. "We'll go out a bit farther." He hauled in the microphone and waved to Max.

The engines roared to life and we headed farther out.

"We should see something here," Adam said after a while.

When the engines were silent, he dropped the microphone into the ocean depths. Twenty minutes went by and still there were no killer whales. Just the occasional school of fish.

My father and I grew increasingly depressed.

"We could still empty Mom's ashes into the ocean," he said.

I shook my head. "It won't be the same. Not without the whales."

Reaching for the silver chain around my neck, I eased the wolf pendant from my shirt. I traced the wolf's head with my fingers, pleading fervently with the Great Spirit to lead us to the whales.

Suddenly, I heard the plaintive song of a killer whale and I saw a plume of water shoot straight up into the air.

"Look!" I cried, pointing toward the horizon.

We stood close together, hypnotized by the spectacular sight of a pod of whales coming up for air. As they drew nearer, my father leaned against the rail, one hand shielding his eyes from the intense sunlight.

"It can't be," he said, shaking his head in disbelief.

Adam smiled at my father. "It's true, Jack. The pod took her in." He laughed lightly. "She's my special project, the reason I'm down here. I'm researching occurrences like this and I have to say, it is very rare."

I was stunned. "That's the same calf we saw?"

"The one who lost her family," my father murmured.

We watched the whales dive below, almost in unison, resurfacing twenty yards from the schooner. I recognized the killer whale that I had once seen, orphaned and alone. I felt an affinity with her. Both of us had been abandoned, left behind. And now we both had found our families.

"She's an adult now," Adam said, interrupting my thoughts. "She just delivered. Two few weeks ago—a female."

Holding onto his arm, I leaned over the rail. When I saw the calf, I chuckled softly, watching her glide next to her mother.

"They look like the ornament you gave me, Adam."

"To remind you of your mother," he said, nodding.

I hissed in a breath. "Quick, Dad! Mom's ashes!"

My father opened the box. Reaching inside, he removed the cloth-covered urn just as the whales plunged into the depths and disappeared below

We waited, holding our breath.

"Do you think they'll come back up?" I asked Adam.

"Look!" my father shouted.

The orca pod was visible a few yards away, but what mesmerized us was the sight of the calf heading straight for us. She circled in front of the schooner, no more than five yards away, eyeing us curiously. Blowing a mist of seawater high into the air, she skimmed against the side of the boat.

WHALE SONG

"Unbelievable," Adam whispered to himself.

We heard the whale crying—singing a soulful melody.

A Whale Song.

My eyes locked on her and I admired the calf's beauty and daring. Stretching down toward the water's surface, my hand dangled and she swam right up to me. I grazed her smooth skin as she passed slowly below me. My emotions overwhelmed me, my memories engulfed me and I tears welled in my eyes.

"Do it now, Dad," I said.

My father tipped the urn and emptied my mother's ashes into the endless ocean. "Until we meet again, my love."

"Goodbye, Mom."

A breeze drifted past us, carrying the ashes into the wind and over the water. My mother had returned to every corner of the earth—becoming part of every living creature. As we watched her ashes melt into the rhythmic waves, I thought that maybe—just maybe—her wish had come true.

Maybe she had become a whale after all.

I reached out my hand as the calf swam past one last time—her open eyes watching me…almost lovingly.

I smiled.

My mother had come to say goodbye.

epilogue

It is said that death begins with the absence of life.

If this is so, then my mother died long before I did what I did. When she slipped into a coma with no hope of surviving or recovering, there was no life left.

It is her *life* that I remember—her laughing smile, her warm embrace and her extraordinary vision. I have learned to use that vision and the intuitiveness of an old but wise Nootka grandmother who once said, *"I may have lost my eyesight, Hai Nai Yu...but I have not lost my vision."*

I embrace my native name, understanding now that I am the *Wise One of the One Who Knows*. The wisdom of the Great Spirit has taught me that we all must do whatever it takes to resolve our past, so that we're able to live fully in our future. I know that with life...comes death...and then life again. The eternal circle—the never-ending story.

But my mother taught me the most important lesson of all.

Forgiveness sets you free.

Introduction to the Discussion Guide

Whale Song holds a very special place in my heart. It was the first book I ever had published. The story had been in my head for two years before I started writing a word. Becoming a published author has always been my deepest desire, my greatest dream. But life got in the way and my dream was put on the back burner.

Many readers have asked me if Whale Song is about me and my life. In some ways it is. There is a lot of me in Sarah. But this is *her* story, not mine. I'm just blessed to be able to share it with you.

Have you ever lost a loved one like Sarah did? I have. I lost my first child at birth and my brother Jason was killed in 2006. He was only 28. When we cleaned out his apartment, we found only a few things of value. One of them was a battered copy of the first edition of Whale Song. Knowing Jason had kept my book helped me say goodbye to my baby brother.

Whale Song is the perfect choice for book clubs and schools! Not only is Whale Song a "beautiful" and "compelling" novel, it has had an emotional impact on many readers and it explores numerous topics, such as life in an isolated town, killer whales, west coast native traditions and legends, the effects of racism, the impact of bullying and abuse, the choice and consequences of assisted death, the depth of a parent's love, and surviving great tragedy.

While this novel was originally marketed mainly for women 30-60 years old, it has now broken all boundaries in age and gender. My youngest reader that I know of is 7 and the oldest is 108. Whale Song has become an international bestseller.

Over the years, since Whale Song was first published in 2003, people of all ages have come to love this coming-of-age tale of family, love, tough challenges, tragedy and forgiveness. I've received numerous emails telling me how Whale Song has changed people's lives, impacted them in ways I never expected. These are my favorite emails, especially the ones from young people.

Whale Song is used as mandatory reading at Community Welcome House, a women and children's shelter in Newnan, Georgia.

WHALE SONG

There's no escaping the fact that today's youth face many of the same issues that Sarah faced—bullying, racism, friendship problems, first love, tragedy and even the death of a loved one.

I was a bullied child. I was the chubby redhead in the back row, who was too shy to speak out and lacked self-confidence. I've experienced bullying just like Sarah did. *Exactly* like Sarah did. I did not fight back physically, though I tried to fight verbally. That rarely works out well. I've experienced racism too. I was a white child living in a small town, and the native Indians weren't too happy about the whites. Like all kids, I had my friendship issues, my first love...and my second, and family problems.

But I survived. It gets better.

If you take nothing away from this guide than those two sentences above, I've fulfilled another goal. To give you hope. I can tell you that if you persevere and focus on what you want out of life, you can get through the bullying, the racism, the loss of loved ones and anything else that comes your way.

There are many messages in Whale Song. Ones about bullying, racism, family and more. I hope you take away the one message that can change your life for the better: *Forgiveness sets you free.*

I'm not saying you have to ignore bullying. If you're a bullied youth, *tell* someone. If no one intervenes, tell someone else. Keep telling people until someone listens and does something.

If you're a bully, I can tell you that you *think* you have power. You don't. That power is an illusion. And illusions disappear eventually. What will you have then? A criminal record? Broken relationships? No future? Being a bully is a choice. So choose not to be one.

Many years ago, long after I was bullied, I saw the girl who bullied me. She was a single mom of two, no job, poor health, and no husband or boyfriend in the picture. I felt sorry for her. She spent so much time during her youth focusing her anger on me that she missed out on her education. She'll most likely be on some kind of social assistance for the rest of her life. Not much of a future, is it?

And I had spent too much time scared of her that I missed out on gaining self-esteem and belief in myself. It took me years to get that. But I did. And when I saw my abuser (because that's what a bully is), I felt nothing but pity for her. And forgiveness.

Why? She didn't know anything else. She had a hard childhood; everyone knew about her family. She was most likely abused or neglected. She was an angry kid. And worst of all, she followed in her family's footsteps of racism towards whites. She learned racism from her parents.

I learned tolerance. And patience, though I wasn't much good at that one.

But I survived. Life DOES get better. I can promise you that.

Life gets better and bigger and more beautiful, with countless possibilities available to you. Life is an adventure, an unwritten story and only you can write those pages for your life. All you need is a dream. Writing was my dream. Thank you for sharing in it.

Thank you for reading my "heart book." I hope you enjoyed it. And if by chance it inspires you in some way, please drop me an email and let me know. cherylktardif@shaw.ca

Sincerely,
Cheryl Kaye Tardif

And now, onto the Discussion Guide...

WHALE SONG DISCUSSION GUIDE
School Edition

(This guide may be scanned & photocopied.)

This discussion guide was designed to help students and teachers get the most out of WHALE SONG. It will give you some insight into how to interpret this work of fiction and the subtle or not-so-subtle messages found in the book. It is divided into four sections: The Story, Bullying, Racism and Death. Teachers are invited to use whichever sections and questions they deem appropriate for their students.

Spoiler Warning: The following questions reveal important details from the novel. You should finish reading WHALE SONG before reading this guide. Teachers of younger readers may decide to overlook the questions on death, in particular the controversial issue, assisted death.

THE STORY:

1. Whale Song is very much a story about love and relationships. What are the different types of love described? How does Sarah's love for her parents change throughout the years? How does her love for Goldie and Nana change? How does her love for Adam change?

2. Sarah's relationships with her new best friend Goldie and Goldie's grandmother Nana is one that many can relate to. Have you ever had a best friend like Goldie, one from a different culture? If so, how did that affect your life? What do you like about Nana? Have you ever had a mentor like Nana?

3. There is much racial tension between Annie and Sarah. Why does Annie act the way she does? How does Sarah's mother help diffuse this situation? What do we learn about her mother? How does racism affect the three girls' lives?

164

4. The legends that Sarah hears from Nana are important to the novel. Why? What do they add? If they were deleted from the novel, would the story have the same effect? Which legend resonates the most with you and your life? Do you think the messages in these legends are applicable for people today?

5. Other than the legends, did you learn anything else about west coast natives and their cultures? What interesting facts about killer whales did you learn that you weren't aware of before? Have you ever gone whale watching? Do you want to go?

6. Sarah begins to see a wolf early on in the novel. What or who does the wolf represent? Why does it become so important in the story?

7. Sarah is bullied by Annie in school. Why do you think Annie picked on Sarah so much? What clues are there in the story that might lead you to conclusions about Annie's life and her "reasons" for being a bully?

8. Sarah's mom told her to find a way to forgive Annie. Do you think this was good advice?

9. Have you ever been bullied? How did that make you feel? Have you ever bullied someone else? Why? What kinds of bullying are there nowadays? How can we as a society (or school) prevent bullying?

10. Sarah becomes friends with Annie shortly after rescuing her from drowning. What changes, and why? What made Annie's life so difficult? Do you think that this story depicts the "normal" life for a young native child in that era? Why does Sarah have such a difficult time understanding Annie's behavior? Have you ever befriended someone who came from a troubled home? How did that impact your life?

11. Why is the story of Fallen Island told?

12. What scenes of foreshadowing are used to suggest Daniella's demise?

13. When Sarah's mother becomes very ill, Sarah overhears her parents arguing. What does her mother ask her father to do? Why?

How would you feel if you overheard your parents discussing death like this?

14. In the hospital, Sarah goes into a fugue-like state after her mother dies. Why?

15. Sarah's father is put in prison. Now that you know the truth, do you think he should have told the authorities that he had nothing to do with his wife's death? Why didn't he? Once Sarah learns the truth, do you think she should have confessed to the authorities? Why?

16. After her father's conviction, why does Sarah harden herself to the point of letting go of everything she loved? Is this a normal reaction?

17. Why did Jack let his daughter go so easily? Why did he say he didn't want her to visit him?

18. Sarah's dreams are often omens about her life. How does her dream about Sisiutl and her mother at the end of the novel reflect her own life?

19. Guilt can make people do things they don't want to do. In what ways does Sarah's guilt control her after her mother's death? How does it control her when she is living with her grandparents? How does it affect her as an adult?

20. When Sarah remembers what really happened, should she have confessed to police? Should she have gone to jail?

21. Sarah learns about forgiveness in many ways. Why is forgiveness so important in her life? Do you agree that "forgiveness sets you free"? Why is forgiveness important to you? Have you ever found it impossible to forgive someone? How has that affected you?

22. Why is the legend of a killer whale being a reincarnated soul so important to this story? At the end, do you think Sarah's mother was coming to say goodbye? How did the scene with Sarah and her father scattering her mother's ashes affect you? How do you think the author wanted you to feel?

23. Many people believe in soul mates, and Sarah and Adam could be described as such. Why do you think they reunited after so many years? Do you believe in soul mates?

24. What messages did you come away with after reading Whale Song?

25. How can a teen benefit from reading Whale Song? How about an adult?

26. How would you rate Whale Song on a scale of 1-5, with 5 being "Excellent"?

27. Is Whale Song a novel you would recommend? Who would you recommend it to?

BULLYING:

1. Have you ever been bullied? If so, how did it make you feel? Do you find it easy to forgive someone who has bullied you? Is there a bully in your life you should forgive now?

2. Have you ever bullied someone? If so, why? What were you feeling at the time? Why did you pick that person to bully?

3. What would you do if someone bullied you today?

4. What would you do if you saw someone being bullied?

5. Why do you think bullies pick on others?

6. How should school officials and teachers deal with a bullying situation?

7. How should parents deal with a bullying situation?

8. What should be the consequences if someone bullies a student on the school grounds?

9. Should a bully be suspended from school?

10. Should a bully be expelled from school?

RACISM:

1. Have you ever been discriminated against because of skin color, race, religion, etc.?

2. Have you ever discriminated against someone else because of skin color, race, religion, etc.?

3. Do you know a racist?

4. Why is racism wrong?

5. What can you do to help stop racism?

DEATH:

1. Have you experienced the death of a family member? If so, how did it make you feel?

2. How can you come to terms with death? How can you move forward?

3. Whale Song explores the controversial issue of assisted death. Do you think people should have the right to die on their terms? Or should only doctors make that call? Discuss your feelings about assisted death. How do you feel about it? Against it completely? Physician-assisted only? And in what cases?

4. What special way can you remember those who have passed away?

5. Does your family have any special traditions for dealing with death?

6. Whale Song is really about life and living life to the fullest. How can you life *your* life to the fullest?

© 2011 Cheryl Kaye Tardif.

Classrooms wishing to engage in a Skype conference with the author can contact Cheryl Kaye Tardif at cherylktardif@shaw.ca

Teachers: I would love to have your input, or that of your students. Feel free to email me at the above address and let me know what you think of this guide. If you use discussion questions that are not listed here that you think should be, I'd be very happy to hear them. ☺ If you teach a senior class and are looking for another novel study, I recommend my thriller THE RIVER, used in many schools, though there is no guide at this time.

Cheryl Kaye Tardif

Cheryl Kaye Tardif is an award-winning, bestselling Canadian suspense author. Her novels include Divine Justice, Children of the Fog, The River, Divine Intervention, and Whale Song, which New York Times bestselling author Luanne Rice calls "a compelling story of love and family and the mysteries of the human heart...a beautiful, haunting novel."

She is currently working on her next thriller, Submerged.

Cheryl also enjoys writing short stories inspired mainly by her author idol Stephen King, and this has resulted in Skeletons in the Closet & Other Creepy Stories (ebook) and Remote Control (novelette ebook).

In 2010 Cheryl detoured into the romance genre with her contemporary romantic suspense debut, Lancelot's Lady, written under the pen name of Cherish D'Angelo.

Booklist raves, "Tardif, already a big hit in Canada...a name to reckon with south of the border."

Cheryl's website: http://www.cherylktardif.com
Official blog: http://www.cherylktardif.blogspot.com
Twitter: http://www.twitter.com/cherylktardif

You can also find Cheryl Kaye Tardif on MySpace, Facebook, Goodreads, Shelfari and LibraryThing, plus other social networks.

IMAJIN BOOKS

Quality fiction beyond your wildest dreams

For your next ebook or paperback purchase, please visit:

www.imajinbooks.com

Made in the USA
Lexington, KY
18 December 2012